The ⟨...⟩ Conspiracy

and

The Candlelight Conspiracy

two stories where good people go
wrong by choosing

The Revenge Option

M.L.Barbani

Warren Publishing, Inc.

Published by Warren Publishing, Inc.
www.warrenpublishing.net

ISBN: 978-1-886057-31-9

Library of Congress Control Number: 2011942425

Printed in the United States of America

The Ring Conspiracy

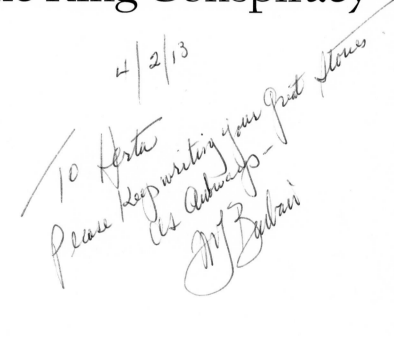

4/2/13

To Herta
Please keep writing your great stories
As always—
[signature]

DEDICATION

To Warren Publishing Inc. President Cathy Brophy, Editor Jere Armen and staff for the final editing of both my stories contained in this volume. Dedication to hard work made it possible. Thank you for making this anthology possible.

To the late fiction writer, teacher, and good friend, Mister Stephan Horvath, who died shortly after reading a short part of my manuscript, The Ring Conspiracy. The literary world will miss that great man who, like Poland's Joseph Conrad had to learn the English language, and then have the brainpower and courage to write stories in their newly acquired tongue. Mister Horvath was born in Budapest, Hungary and studied at Eotvos Lorant University. Mister Horvath became a U.S. citizen in 1965. He published his novel, 'Picara' in 2008. Also by S.I. Horvath, 'Caged Metal Feathers'.

To all Pamlico Writer's Group, Washington, N.Carolina past and present members, for their critiques during my journey to write fiction and make it good action/adventure trips.

I thank you all.

PROLOGUE

The expansive lawn within the estate of Sir Henry Ethan Johnson's country home, southwest of London was an ideal place for an active child to release built-up energy. The dark-haired, good-looking ten-year-old boy, Jonathon Malcolm Johnson, the spoiled son of the wealthy industrialist, played rough and tumble with the horde of other family boys and girls of similar age.

"Whoever finds the ring gets a sweet," yelled an older boy. "Let's go, let's go", cheered the children as a half dozen of them scattered in search of the multi-colored toy ring hidden among the many shrubs surrounding the estate. Parents, aunts and uncles took quick peeks out the windows in half-hearted supervision of their progeny.

"My goodness, they do seem to play on the rough side, all for a useless toy," remarked one of the mothers.

"Oh, let them at it. Give them the room they need to expend their energies. Play hard, and learn what a tough world this is at an early age. I only wish I were their age again," said a middle-aged uncle reclined in a comfortable stuffed chair, nursing a glass of Port and smoking a Cuban cigar.

"Ha!" a short laugh echoed from another relative.

Outside, though the sun was shining, the late May temperature was rather cool for this time of the year. No matter, the game was on and all the children participated in the hunt. After a time, there came an excited announcement.

"I found it! I found it!" a boy in front of Jonathon yelled, holding the ring as he emerged from the green shrubs.

Jonathon's eyebrows formed into an ugly frown. "But I saw it first," he said.

"No, you did not. I saw it and I picked it up."

"No, no, no. You cheated," was Jonathon's strong reply. "So give it here, it belongs to me, and I get the sweet," he screamed and snatched the toy ring from his younger cousin, Trevor Zelcorr II.

Before young Trevor could muster a reply, he fell to the ground under a sadistic attack of brutal kicks and punches from Jonathon Malcolm Johnson. Squeals and yells broke out as the group came together and witnessed the ugly beating. Several parents noted the commotion and hurried outside to intervene. In the end, it was Jonathon standing, proudly holding his prize high over his head.

"I found the hidden ring, it's mine, and I get the sweet." He never took his eyes off the fallen boy.

Trevor, the injured one, whimpering with tears streaming down his face, walked hand-in-hand with his mother to the house. The other children formed a group and silently denounced Jonathon for his perfidious cheating and abusive assault on his smaller relative, Trevor. Jonathon just smiled. *Stupid cousin, the ring is mine!*

A lavish lunch served in the Johnson estate home changed the atmosphere to a festive afternoon. However, Trevor Zelcorr II, who had suffered the blows from Jonathon, now felt completely humiliated and distraught, more from the embarrassment rather from the painful attack. He glared at Jonathon sitting almost across from him. *I'll get you Jonathon, you lying, cheating thief, I'll get even with you, I will.*

CHAPTER 1

Sir Jonathon Malcolm Johnson, age thirty-nine, was having a carefree evening enjoying the company of his new girlfriend, Miss Mary Melton Avery. They dined at the Yorkshire Arms restaurant in the fashionable part of London's West End. They each ordered the roast duck with fresh vegetables, and were completely satisfied with their meals. The restaurant was, more often than not, full of patrons, but Sir Jon, as his close friends called him, always had a reserved table in a quiet alcove. The restaurant provided first-class furnishings with deep red, soft velvet drapes covering the huge tall windows that shut out the sights and sounds of the outside world. A string quartet played soft background music in a recess away from the dining customers.

During the dessert phase, Jonathon and Mary fed each other juicy bits of rum-soaked wedges of moist, fresh cake, using delicate fingertip control. It was a joyful occasion, and the two were having a grand time. Jonathon paid the bill after they had indulged in small cups of Espresso coffee and the finest Cognac the restaurant had to offer.

Sir Jonathon looked at his hands and said, "Will you excuse me, Mary? I am afraid I have been a bit of a pig with my fingers. I'll just be a minute to clean up some."

"Good idea. I'll do the same and meet you at the front door."

"Excellent," he replied.

They got up and weaved their way between the crowded tables. Jonathon paused to greet and talk to several dining patrons. Mary quickly descended the carpeted spiral stairway to the lower floor—equally well appointed, with oil-polished, dark wood paneling and elegant drapery. A few select pieces of fine art hung tastefully interspersed along the walls. Entering the brightly lit Gents room, Mary realized her error, said "Oops, sorry," turned, and hurried for the Ladies room. The attendant gave a nod, and continued with his duties. Meanwhile, Jonathon eventually descended the same stairway. He entered the Gents room where Sal Chapman, the attendant, greeted him.

"Good evening, Sir Jonathon," he said while handing him a fresh hand towel as was customary with each patron.

"And a good evening to you, Sal. I could use a bit of a clean-up."

Jonathon handed his overcoat to the attendant, then turned and stepped to the nearest marble-top washbasin, tossing the hand towel over what looked like a very expensive ring, with rows of diamonds surrounding a larger, central precious gemstone. It now lay hidden underneath his towel.

Jonathon, a well-built man standing just under six feet and sporting an expensive suit, leaned forward to inspect his near-handsome face in the large mirror. He then proceeded to wash his hands. When Sal turned away, Jonathon took a quick peek at him. *No problem: he had not noticed the ring underneath my hand towel. Surely, he would have said something. Pretty slick, old boy,* he congratulated himself as he straightened up at the sink and admired his stealthy skill. He carefully picked up the towel with the now passenger ring, and with care, he gently wiped his moist hands dry.

"You know, Sal, I have a hobby collecting these small hand towels. Rather silly, I suspect, but to each his own, eh? I have hand towels from some of the best restaurants in the world. I do declare, it will be quite a large collection indeed. Uh, may I have this one?"

"Oh, yes of course; but I'll get you a clean one." He moved to a small table that held a neat stack of hand towels, small-prepackaged soap bars and other grooming items.

"That won't be necessary, Sal; I'll just fold this one and put it in my coat pocket here." He then extracted a wallet from the inside pocket of his jacket, pulled out a five-pound note, and handed it to Sal.

"That won't be necessary, Sir Jonathon; we have plenty of towels for our guests."

"Oh, but I insist," and he gently forced the note into Sal's hand.

"Well then, thank you, sir."

Jonathon brushed back a few grey hairs, gave a nod to a mirror, and said, "And I thank you, Sal. It is always a pleasure to see you. Good night now."

With that last exchange, the ring rode comfortably within the folds of the restaurant's linen, safely tucked in Sir Jonathon's coat pocket.

On his way up the spiral stairway, a man descending almost bumped into Jonathon, his direction: the Gents room. He quickly entered, and in a strained and excited voice called out, "I was here a few minutes ago, and I believe I left my ring on that sink top."

"But, sir, you must be mistaken," exclaimed Sal. "As you can see," he extended an open hand, "there is no ring here at any wash basin."

CHAPTER 2

The man at the door leaned on the call button of the Johnson estate home and hoped for a quick, positive response. He shifted his feet side to side and shoved his hands deep into his coat pockets to combat the chilly night air. Soon, the large door opened on well-oiled hinges. Michael Harlington, the able-bodied, fifty-one-year-old household butler blocking the way forward, looked at the man whose dress was quite common.

"May I help you?" he asked, giving the outsider a quick once over.

"I would like to see the master of the house, if it's not too much trouble."

"May I have your name and the purpose of your visit?"

"Oi, not to worry ol' man, just tell Sir Jonathon that Sal Chapman is 'ere to see him—*personally*—on an important and confidential matter." Michael, a good judge of character, could tell the solidly built man in front of him was about the same age as Sir Jonathon, perhaps a bit younger, and exhibited an air of steadfastness. After a short pause, Michael said, "Won't you step inside and wait a moment? I'll see if Sir Jonathon is free to receive visitors." Sal stepped into the warm foyer, and bobbed his head in appreciation of the expensive furnishings lining both sides of the opulent hallway—a finer side of life, to be sure.

Presently, Michael reappeared and motioned with a wave of his hand. "Would you step this way; Sir Jonathon will see you now." Sal followed Michael to a huge double door and gained admittance into the room. The light from several small antique wall lamps, although somewhat dim, made the large room out to be a handsome, well-stocked library. Several rolling, polished wooden ladders provided access to bookshelves that reached close to the ceiling. Volumes occupied most of three wall shelves. Sir Jonathon stood at the far end behind a bar that would rival that of any refined pub in England.

"Ah, there you are, Sal. How are you, and would you care for a drink?"

After a thoughtful pause, Sal answered in quick London slang, "Oi, don't mind if I do. A *frisky* would go down nicely now." Jonathon smiled, poured a good amount into a wide-mouth, heavy glass and placed it on the bar top with a nod to his unwelcomed guest. Sal approached the bar and the two men faced each other.

Sal raised the glass in a salute, and downed a good portion. "Ah, that's a fine *frisky*—if one can afford it, mind you," while wiping his full mustache with the back of his hand.

"Surely you didn't come to see me to sample and judge my whiskey, or to impress me with your London slang, now did you, Sal?"

"Well now, a few practiced lines of fine English words to get a job, and a bob or two. . . I'll leave the rest to your imagination, eh?"

"I say, your transformation from Cockney to culture, and back again, is quite remarkable," answered Jonathon.

With a shrug of his shoulders, Sal asked, "'Ave you got a *fag*, by chance?" Jonathon turned his head and gave a quick nod to the other end of the bar. Sal approached a well-made, small wooden box, flipped the lid up and extracted a handful of cigarettes. He put one to his lips and struck an accompanying match with his thumbnail. He blew it out and tossed it onto the bar top, purposely missing a large ashtray. He pocketed the remaining fags into his knee-length, scruffy coat.

Cheeky bastard, thought Jonathon, *so you want to play games, eh?*

"Let's quit fencing, Sal, and tell me what's on your mind." Sal returned to Jonathon, tilted his head back and exhaled a cloud of smoke up to the high ceiling.

"Simply put, you pinched something of mine, and I want it back. Is that clear enough for ya?"

"Not really, just what are you referring to?"

"Don't take me for a fool, Jonathon. You must 'ave known I had me eye on that ring. I was about to claim it when you walked into me Gents room and snatched it."

"Ah, the ring—and you're assuming I took it."

7

"DON'T . . . play games with me, Jonathon," Sal's voice took on a strong aggressive tone. "The ring was gone when you left the room. It doesn't take a Sherlock to figure that out."

"First of all, Sal, that ring looked very expensive and quite valuable, to say the least. I sincerely doubt you could afford such a purchase on your wages. Therefore, I conclude, it is not yours but mine, and possession is nine-tenths of the law. Furthermore, I do plan to track down the owner and return it as soon as possible," he lied. Sal placed both hands on the edge of the bar giving it a nasty tug and leaned closer to Jonathon.

"Ya really don't know who you're talking to, do you? I'll bet you never heard of Sal the Savage Chapman in the boxing world, 'ave you now? I could drop your rich arse in less than ten seconds; so don't mess with me!"

"Well now, that presents an interesting matchup indeed, brawn against brains." Undaunted by the aggrieved tone, Jonathan held his ground and stared at his potential opponent.

I'll squash you like a bug my friend, or can get it done professionally; any way you like it.

"What do you suggest to settle this dispute?" asked Jonathon. Sal thought for a moment then challenged, "I'll give you till tomorrow night to think about it. Let's meet behind the dosshouse in Limehouse district at eleven. Be there, and we will settle up. Oh, bring the ring, or regret the consequences. But I'd rather see it done peacefully, and then all's forgiven and forgotten."

"DONE! said the king," as Jonathon let out a short laugh and raised a whiskey glass to salute his antagonist. Without another word, Sal glared at Jonathon and stubbed his cigarette on the polished bar-top right in front of him. He punctuated the insult by tossing the burned stub at the ashtray—missing it, of course. He then turned and walked to the same doors through which he had entered. Before leaving, he faced Jonathon and mocked aloud, "A large collection of restaurant towels? Now 'ere's a good one. HA! Nice try, ol' man, but you don't get a sweet!" With that, Sal stormed out of the room, leaving a large echo from the slammed door in his wake. Sir Jonathon simply stood behind the bar staring at the closed door, his gut, his eyes, tingling with rage.

You slimy, insulting bastard, thought Jonathon as he reached for the telephone.

CHAPTER 3

"I want him stomped on, pleading and bleeding! I want him hurt and hurt bad! I want him suffering and begging for mercy," Jonathon screamed into the phone. His once handsome face now contorted with malice and vengefulness. His breathing labored and spittle sprayed the telephone mouthpiece. Finally he regained control, and instructed, "Don't kill him; I will not tolerate a murder investigation linking me to that slob. But make sure he visits the hospital for a lengthy and painful stay." Using some of his own London slang terms, he ordered, *"Do him over—proper!"*

After giving the time and directions to the party at the end of the connection, he slammed the phone down. Tossing his head back, he smoothed down his prematurely graying hair and tried to calm down.

Jonathon retreated to his desk a few yards from the bar, opened a locked drawer and withdrew a flat, glass plate with a powdery substance all lined in rows.

"Michael!" Jonathon shouted, as the blood vessels gorged and popped along his temples and neck.

"Bring whatever necessary to clean up the mess that wind-bag caused to my bar. He will pay for his insults and actions—just like any other who threaten me."

CHAPTER 4

The night wind whipped around the corner of the darkened alleyway, bringing with it a chill that caused the two men to pull up their coat collars as they waited for their prey to arrive. The glowing ember of a cigarette was the only light at this end of the dosshouse. Soon, another man walking the darkened pavement slowly approached. He was wearing a short, sturdy coat with his collar also turned up. A wool cap pulled down to eyebrow level kept his head warm. As he neared the two men leaning against the wall, one of them called out, "Oi, 'ave ya got a fag, mate?" Sal the Savage pulled up close and muttered something under his breath. He offered a cigarette, and cupped a flaming match in both hands in an offer to light the damn thing so he could be on his way. It was a wrong move.

With his hands occupied, and arms outstretched, he did not see the body punch coming; a left hook to his ribs brought forth an "Uruh" sound from Sal. The blow took his breath and he sank to one knee. The other assailant rushed in and landed a downward right cross to Sal's jaw that sent him falling face down onto the dirty pavement. Too bad it wasn't a knockout punch. By instinct, Sal rolled on to his back and whipped out a vicious kick that, by luck, connected with the leg of one of his attackers. He went down while Sal got up quickly and recovered from the previous blows. He thanked God for his former boxing training, and snapped out a left jab at the face coming toward him. *Crunch*, went the nose. With the attacker's hands going to nursing his painful, bleeding snout, Sal sent another punch to the bloke's solar plexus. The force of that blow penetrated through the heavy clothing of the attacker, causing him to weaken and lose his breath. Sal followed up with a solid left hook to the kidney area. This bloke went down hard. However, the other attacker, who was on one knee, sprang up and charged into Sal, pinning him hard against the doss house wall. With only one option left, Sal head-butted the ugly face in front of him. When the arms released Sal, he set up a one, two, three punch combination that sent the attacker down almost on top of the other assailant. Neither decided, nor tried, to get up.

Regaining his breath and standing over his attackers, Sal Chapman bent down, picked up his cap, slapped it to his pant leg, and adjusted it to his head. In a low firm voice he said, "You blokes are pathetic; next time, tell Sir Jonathon to send in the Royal Marines."

CHAPTER 5

It had been two days since Jonathon had turned his Foundry thugs loose on Sal. He was furious that the report was not what he had wanted to hear.

The Johnson Foundry was one of many plants owned by the sole survivor, Sir Jonathon Malcolm Johnson. Its production supplied many finished iron and heavy steel mechanisms for various industries in Europe and the Middle East. He was indeed obsessed with importance by the *Sir OBE* title recommended by the government, then signed and issued by the Queen. Although Sir Jonathon occupied a privileged seat among the nation's highest echelons of society, he also harbored a willingness to commit crimes against that same social order with his hidden philosophy toward life: *I have a need for GREED.*

Now sitting with his fingers laced together, he was staring at the lavish breakfast plate in front of him. Although the weather outside was agreeable, he chose to remain on the glass-enclosed patio at the back of his estate home. Moreover, despite the view of the outstanding garden with budding flowers of all species, Jonathon was locked in a dark and foul mood.

"And a good morning to you, Jon," said Mary as she cheerfully approached and took a chair at the breakfast table. Mary was beautiful, but not *movie star* beautiful. However, her face could have graced many magazine covers, if she had pursued that path of profession. With clean features, and a slender curvy body to match, she certainly would be labeled a trophy wife indeed.

"Umm, this looks fabulous and appetizing, but you look like you lost your favorite toy. What's wrong, Jon?"

Jonathon picked up his fork, played with the Eggs Benedict, and ignored her question. She picked up her utensils and pleaded, "Now, Jon, I can see something is bothering you. Come on, talk to me."

13

"NO, damn it, it's a private affair," he yelled while striking the tabletop with a clenched fist.

His sudden, violent outburst startled Mary, causing her to drop her knife and fork. She recovered from her initial shock, took a breath, and quietly asked, "Another woman, perhaps?"

"You would be terribly wrong thinking that, Mary," he answered in an apologetic tone and taking her hand. "I'm sorry for losing my temper. Sometimes it . . . Please forgive me."

"Then come clean, or we're both going to spoil a perfectly splendid breakfast."

"Very well, if you're going to insist," Jonathon relented, raising his head, and took a deep breath. "I'm locked in a battle with the Gents Room attendant at the Yorkshire Arms restaurant. That blackguard lied and accused me of committing a most ugly and terrible thing."

"Oh, him," said Mary as she took a small bite of her eggs.

Surprised, Jonathon stirred and questioned, "What do you mean *him*? Do you know Sal Chapman?"

"Well I should: he's my uncle."

"What? Your uncle?"

"Why, yes, I helped him get the job at that restaurant. What has that habitual liar done now?"

Jonathon now wore a troubled look on his face. *How am I going to explain this to Mary? I certainly can't tell her the truth. Lucky I hadn't given the ring to her yet. Think . . . think, damn you!*

He straightened up and with complete composure—something he always accomplished easily—calmly said, "Actually, it isn't all that serious. I hope to resolve the problem soon. Please, promise me you will not get involved. It is just a personal matter that I can cope with. Now, let's finish our breakfast and forget that incident." He then added, "You are right, it would be a shameful waste to ruin a perfectly decent meal. Besides, my cook would severely scold me straight away."

His forced attempt at a light-hearted conclusion did not put Mary totally at ease, no indeed. *She already knew about the event that had taken place in the Gents room.*

CHAPTER 6

Twenty laps around the oblong circle on the second floor of the Stay Fit Health Club seemed to be about right. Sweat poured from seemingly every pore in the fairly well-defined body of Trevor Zelcorr II. From here, he would normally step into the wide-open space adjacent to the run-lane for a torturous martial arts session before heading for his reward of a soothing and relaxing massage, followed by a skin care treatment by the club's professional. However, today's physical workout had to be abbreviated because of the looming workload at his father's law practice, Zelcorr and Son.

From boyhood, Trevor had been weak and sickly, and always tormented by the tough boys. His attitude changed during his university years at Oxford, where he learned to be more assertive, physically able to challenge any adversary, and determined to win a spot on the school's Rugby club. Hard as he had tried, though physically fit now, he did not make the cut. Instead of being down and out, that disappointment doubled Trevor's determination to improve, and had given him a new interpretation of the Rugby club's motto, YOU CAN!
You . . . *bloody well . . .* **can.**
Today, at age forty, Trevor was a successful partner in his father's law firm. He, happily married, had fathered two children, a boy and a girl. They lived in a fashionable home in a wealthy neighborhood not far from Chancery Lane. Although content with his life, Trevor harbored a dark and disturbing obsession deep within his soul. He knew he must act soon or all would be lost. He had to keep working, keep digging, keep after his investigators, and get to the whole truth. *I must have proof to indict and successfully prosecute the bastard!*

15

CHAPTER 7

Mary left the Johnson house with a promise not to get involved in the dispute between Sal and Jonathon. She made that promise but shrugged it off with the expression, *Not to worry.*

Meanwhile, Jonathon left the patio area and entered the library, where Michael held the telephone and announced, "There is a phone call for you, sir."

"Who is it?"

"I'm not sure, sir, but I think it's that man called Sal."

"Damn it, I've told you a dozen times, I don't speak to anyone on the telephone unless I know his or her name," said Jonathon in a most displeased voice.

"Yes, sir, quite right; it won't happen again." Jonathon snatched the phone from Michael's hand and waited for him to leave the room before answering the caller.

"Hello, who is this?" Jonathon spoke into the handset.

"And a good morning to you, Jonathon. I do hope you've recovered from the unpleasant news your blokes had to report. You know, I thought you were a smart gent, but you proved to be a dumb sonofabitch with no guts at all."

"You had your fun, Sal, now what is it you want?"

"Want? Want?" mocked Sal. "What I want is the bleedin' ring, Jonathon—*and* a hundred thousand pounds for me troubles, or I go to Scotland Yard with me story. That's what I want, ya bloody wanker!"

Jonathon had not expected that answer, especially the extortion of a hundred thousand pounds. His mind raced for a solution and, by a stroke of luck and quick thinking, he found it: *Counter-attack.*

"How dare you threaten ME! Go ahead, you washed-up, punch-drunk bum. Go ahead. . . I dare you! Go to the police or whoever. Whose word do you think they will believe—yours, against mine? By god, I'll make sure, with my connections, they'll put you away for a very long time, you miserable, disgusting bastard."

Sal was shocked at the sudden outburst from Jonathon. In fact, he felt that he had lost his seemingly strong hand in this confrontation. Now he was at a disadvantage. Sal struggled for a quick answer, but unable to come up with something clever and not wanting to make a stupid response, he merely quietly replaced the telephone onto its base.

"Hello, hello?" The connection was dead. Jonathon, in a sudden state of physical and mental rage, glared at the phone in his hand. *"How dare you hang up on me? Me, with a title of Sir, signed by the Queen! You . . . you . . . common piece of crud!"* He hurled the phone across the room with such force that the connecting cable separated from the wall box, leaving behind a clatter of bell sounds and a loss of further telephone service for the rest of this day, at the least.

Jonathon tilted his head up and let out a howl, then a scream, and ending with a flood of curse words all strung together. His eyes bulged; his head ached with a fierce pain at the base of his skull. His arms flexed; his hands doubled into fists. Stumbling backward into a soft lounge chair, he tried to regain his breath, while his heart rate was that of a runaway beast galloping uphill to confront an enemy. His jaw locked up; his teeth clenched. *Get a grip, damn it. Slow down. Lord, I need a drink, and to . . . think!*

Frantic and exhausted, he mumbled, "Damn it, I need my stash."

CHAPTER 8

The twelve-meter tugboat named *Swamp Donkey* was hauling two crates of varying dimensions, off-loaded from a freighter registered in the Middle East. The cargo labeled for the Johnson Company warehouse was bound for that address even at this late hour. The tug slowly motored up the Thames estuary towards London, encountering some small waves, but little river traffic. Now settled into calm waters, the tug cruised past the Tower of London and the Houses of Parliament.

The *Swamp Donkey* eased into Cheswick Pier and tied up for the night. The captain notified Port Control even at this late hour that it had the standard documentation and usual shipment for the Johnson Company. The port authorities anticipated no problems as this routine delivery for the Johnson Company was repeated in an orderly practice many times during the year.

Meanwhile, surveillance team number two noted the nighttime off-loading and the two crates carried into a local Johnson-owned warehouse within the port property. The surveillance team, parked a block away, figured they finally had gotten a break, perhaps a good lead into Johnson Company affairs of questionable business practice.

"Hello, Mister Zelcorr, this is Knobby and Mick of team number two. Sorry to call on you so late at night, but I think we may have a lead on the Johnson affair. Either way, I thought you'd like to know."

Trevor's hand gripped the phone while reaching for paper and pen as it was still too early for him to call it a night.

"Yes, go ahead; tell me what you found out."

"As you may know, we were parked in a position this week to monitor the Johnson warehouse at Cheswick Pier. After observing this night's activity at the Port Control building, we observed two crates being off-loaded from a tug and hauled to the Johnson warehouse. It may be nothing because these deliveries happen many times during the year.

But never at night that we know of. Kind of perks your interest, eh, what?"

"Good work, lads. I'm glad you've kept your eyes open. Make sure you give the details of those crates to the next team taking your place. I don't want the crates slipping out of sight and not knowing their contents or destination. Meet me at our conference room in the morning for further details and for new procedures to implement."

"Roger, copy that, Mister Zelcorr. We'll keep the next team informed. See you tomorrow. Good night, sir." Surveillance team number two shared a congratulatory handshake and prepared to meet the next team. All team investigators were certified graduates of North London Security Academy and licensed to operate within their prescribed jurisdiction. Excitement was in the air as visions of solving a mystery stirred team number two.

CHAPTER 9

The next morning Trevor met with Knobby and Mick in the law firm's conference room. Knobby Gault, a big beefy man, strong as a bull and not an ounce of humor in his muscular frame, sat comfortably with his legs outstretched, his hands clasped behind his head. Young Mick Andrews, a lanky undersized local with flaming red hair and an enthusiastic yearning to get things done, quite the opposite, sat with his arms on the table giving Trevor his complete attention.

The drapes were partially drawn, and the conference table was more than adequate to support a dozen people and their clients. A secretary brought in hot tea for the three men sitting in polished-wood and leather chairs.

"Right now, can you describe the crates that were off-loaded last night?" asked Trevor.

Knobby, the older of the two investigators, sat up and replied, "I'd say one crate was about one meter square, and the other perhaps two meter square and built of wood—rather sturdy, I suspect." He glanced at Mick who confirmed the limited description with a nod of his head.

"We could have taken some photos from our position, but the night would have obscured most details," injected the younger investigator.

"Word on the street confirms quite a lot of drugs, mostly cocaine, gets out of that warehouse. However, there are other companies who rent space in that building, and we still don't know by whom, or how the drugs get distributed into the community," said Trevor as he sipped the last of his tea. Drumming his fingertips on the polished tabletop he said, "Damn it, I'll have to get someone into that warehouse for a look-see. I'll need shipping labels, cargo data, whatever info that can be lifted from those wooden boxes. Most of all, I need solid confirmation that the crates were indeed assigned to the Johnson company—or not."

"I'll do it sir, if you can get me in there." Twenty-three-year-old Mick almost shouted as he stood up from his chair. "I know that area of Cheswick. My father used to have a boat tied up there, and I still have a few friends from that neighborhood." He sat down before Knobby could volunteer his own response. Knobby smiled, *All right, laddie, you will get your chance if Trevor agrees. Only pray that you can handle what you're getting into.*

CHAPTER 10

After several high-level phone calls made from the law firm of Zelcorr and Son, Mick Andrews was hired as a warehouseman-apprentice working at the Johnson depot and pulled a night-shift for his training period. His duties were to assist other experienced warehousemen in locating, storing, and moving crates around the various sections of the indoor facility. This allowed him some freedom to scout and become familiar with the various loads within the building.

Having busied himself with toting a shop-supplied clipboard, Mick casually made honest-to-goodness notes during his work-related rounds within the warehouse. Unknown to all, a hidden, micro-digital audio recorder in his buttoned-down shirt pocket captured all his spoken words. It was a technique he had learned and carried out during his stint as a private investigator working for the Zelcorr law firm. This temporary assignment in the warehouse was an exciting adventure that would look good on his short resume.

Yes sir, now this is real investigative work, better than surveillance from a smelly car, Mick thought to himself.

On his second night in the warehouse, he succeeded in finding the two crates that had been off-loaded from the tugboat. They were located in a shadowy area deep within the building, apart from a large consignment of crates. He quickly took down notes from the shipping labels and quietly spoke into his recorder just before leaving to end his shift. Just then, two burly warehousemen came down the semi-darkened aisle and questioned Mick.

"'Ere now, what you doin' 'angin' round these two crates?" Completely surprised by the approaching men, Mick dropped his clipboard, picked it up and turned away from them in a move that anticipated an escape. He realized his mistake as both men reached out and yanked him off his feet. One of them held Mick with a cargo hook;

its eight-inch metal hook encircled Mick's arm up close to his armpit. If he struggled, the sharp tip would cause him serious injury.

The lead warehouseman took the clipboard and examined its contents. He read Mick's notes slowly, then looked up and said to his mate, "Hook 'im good." With a twist of the wooden handle, the hook dug into Mick's upper arm, which caused him to yell out in pain.

"Shut 'im up now," whispered the leader. With Mick's left hand up trying to dislodge the hook, his tortured face was an easy target. A big fist smashed into Mick's mouth and he fell to the dirty floor. Blood flowed from his split lips and from the cargo hook's puncture. The man with the hook released it, and hit Mick on the side of his head with the blunt side of the tool. Although bleeding and punished by pain, he remained conscious, but had difficulty stifling his tortured moans and groans.

"Blimey, look 'ere." The warehouseman tapped at the notes on the clipboard. "He must know something 'bout our stuff. This could be dangerous for all of us." At that moment, another figure appeared and approached the duo. He took the clipboard from the warehouseman for his own examination. A frown on his face was his only expression. Mick, lying on his back, looked up at the new man facing him. He raised his hands a bit and muttered, "Please, plea—"

"Hush, laddie, it's all right. Be quiet now." Knobby Gault knelt down and gently took Mick's head in his hands. He repeated, "It's all over now—be still."

With a violent, sharp twist, Knobby's strong hands snapped the spinal cord in Mick's neck. The young investigator died; his bloody mouth open, his eyes rolled back in his head.

Knobby got up and without emotion ordered, "Rock him down good, and dump him in the river."

The two warehousemen threw a tarp over the lifeless body and began to roll him up.

"Wait." Knobby reached into the tarp, tore Mick's shirt pocket down to expose and remove the small audio recorder. "Toss that clipboard in," pointing to the tarp, "and don't forget to clean up this blood. I'll take care o' this recorder."

CHAPTER 11

Three days later, Chief Inspector Albert LaGrange of the Metropolitan Police, Thames Division, sat opposite Trevor Zelcorr as they shared what information there was at hand to continue the investigation into the death of Mick Andrews. LaGrange had not removed his open overcoat and sat in front of his friend. His goatee and bushy eyebrows partially hid a wise and matured face that commanded attention. Inspector LaGrange, with his twenty-two years' experience in the Metropolitan Police, was supervising this MIT team in the investigation of the deceased Mick Andrews.

Trevor had read the initial news report of an unidentified body fished out of the Thames, but had had no knowledge of its identity—until now.

"It can't be true." Trevor's words were slow, his demeanor shaken by the now identified body.

"I'm afraid it's all too true," confessed LaGrange.

"He was sitting right here with his partner, Knobby Gault, just a few days ago. I arranged for Mick to work at the Johnson warehouse on a temporary basis. It's my fault, because I had suspicions of criminal activity originating from that building." Inspector LaGrange pulled out his notebook and began to reveal some of its contents.

"Our investigation and follow-up autopsy confirmed Mick Andrews was murdered and dumped into the Thames. First, the weights in his pockets were not heavy enough to keep the body under water. Moreover, the autopsy concluded that he had a puncture wound, split lips, a bad injury to his head, and a broken neck. That is not a nice way to die. His shopcoat bore the name of the Johnson warehouse at Cheswick, which confirms your statements. Now, can you tell me what Mister Andrews, as a private investigator working for your firm, may have uncovered? Do you have evidence of any criminal activity emanating from that particular building?"

"I'm afraid that, at this point, you have a great deal more information than I, Inspector. I have my suspicions, of course, but no proof whatsoever."

"What of his partner, Knobby Gault?" asked LaGrange.

"Knobby was put on hold, so to speak. He was not assigned to the warehouse, and was told to make himself available only if needed. I have no reason to believe he was involved in that hideous attack. Those two were good friends and worked well together, as far as I know."

"Yes, well, I've already questioned Knobby, and he has an alibi confirmed by his roommate for the night of the murder. However, I intend to query them further in that regard." Indicating that he had to leave, Inspector LaGrange got up and declared, "I have more work to do. We have been friends a long time, Trevor. I'm sorry this affair affects you. If there is anything, any occurrence before the attack that may shed some light on the killer, you will let me know, correct?"

"Without a doubt, Albert, and, please, find and nail that murdering blackguard to the wall." They shook hands and LaGrange went to the door. He paused, tapped a finger to his chin several times, turned and addressed Trevor. "About the body: funny thing about his shirt pocket being ripped down like that, the pocket button also missing. I cannot imagine any kind of fish doing that. And for what purpose? Do you have any ideas along those lines?"

"I am sorry, Inspector, I haven't a clue."

"All right then, should you hear or remember anything, do give me a ring. Good day, Trevor, and when this is all over, we'll have a drink and a bite of dinner together." With that he buttoned his overcoat, donned his hat, gave a quick wave to his friend, and left the Zelcorr law office.

An inner jolt shook Trevor's body after LaGrange departed. He paced the room, seemingly confused, puzzled, something nagging deep within his psyche.

CHAPTER 12

At eleven o'clock that evening, Elizabeth Zelcorr softly knocked, then entered Trevor's study. She was dressed in her nightclothes, which suited her well-formed, attractive body. She indeed loved her husband and longed for a more intimate relationship with him. However, they had grown apart, but she continued to make amends.

Trevor was on his feet, still in his day clothes and staring out the window as if trying to pull an act of contrition out of the clear night sky. How could he have made such a blunder in allowing young Mick Andrews to be placed in that Johnson warehouse without backup?

"Trevor, it's late. Won't you come to bed now?"

Elizabeth's soft words broke his concentrated spell.

Trevor turned from the window, slammed a fist into an open hand, and in anguish said, "It was me. It's my fault!"

"Darling, I've known about your obsession with punishing Sir Jonathon for quite some time now. Don't you see the harm that this lengthy pursuit is causing? It has consumed your sense of fair play, and it has driven a wedge between us. Please, Trev, let the past go. What happened between you and Jonathon was a long, long, time ago."

Trevor shook his head, turned and looked at his wife. His face showed the strain of this day's news, but his eyes were clear and his voice steady.

"No, no, no, Beth; this is not about that louse, that slimy dirt-bag Jonathon. You've read the recent papers: it's about the death of that young investigator, Mick Andrews. I am responsible for his tragic death. I hired him. I sent him to that warehouse. And by **God**, it's my fault that he's dead."

"Trevor, that was NOT your fault. Mick knew there were some dangers in his chosen profession. You did not force or order him to that warehouse. I daresay he volunteered, true? Please don't think along those self-punishing lines, Trev. Stop torturing yourself." With a final sigh and a shrug of her shoulders, Elizabeth stepped away. "It is very late, Trev, I'm going to bed. Darling, please do come up soon."

After she left, quietly closing the door, Trevor returned to gaze out of the window. His mind reeled, and then he settled his thinking with logically considered deductions: *All right then, if not my fault, then whose? Who could have done that to Mick? And why? What was it LaGrange said about the body? What was it? It's driving me— wait!* Trevor's body went into an alert state; his fingertips danced along his forehead, then he stood perfectly still as if in a trance.

By Jove! That's it: the torn shirt pocket! No fish could . . . But who, for what? After a short pause: *By Thunder, I've got it! The audio recorder, they both carried one on duty. Both of them . . . Damn him, it had to be Knobby Gault.*

CHAPTER 13

"I'm getting pretty sick and tired of you incompetent people working for me. When are you blokes going to do something right? Have you an intelligent answer for me, or any intelligence at all? —NO! Do not speak. Just keep your mouth shut for now." Jonathon, in an agitated mood, paced the floor around the seated big, bad Knobby Gault, who sat comfortably in a leather club chair in the library at the estate of Sir Jonathon Malcolm Johnson. Knobby, in his arrogance, showed no fear of the raging man periodically appearing in his view.

Jonathon kept flipping Mick's digital voice recorder in the air as if it were a small coin. He had previously snorted a couple lines of cocaine and fortified his addiction with a good deal of alcohol. His insides were roaring, his brain a jangled web of fiery impulses. He felt invincible! Gone was the intelligent, healthy, and successful industrialist (OBE no less) who would conquer all obstacles in his path to become the supreme ruler of the drug trade in the United Kingdom. His body now tingled with energy, certainly and inevitably leading him to bizarre, erratic, and, as would soon be discovered, violent behavior.

His addiction to the drugs cocaine and heroin certainly altered his personality from Jekyll to Hyde and back. Jonathon kept circling Knobby Gault, who now became quite nervous, especially so when he noted the elderly, but physically fit butler, Michael, standing quietly among the shadows of the great room.

Jonathon paused behind Knobby, put the recorder in his pocket, then removed a length of strong rope from his jacket. He quickly looped it over Knobby's head and drew it up tight around his throat. At first Knobby sat up, then the noose slackened, which relaxed Knobby's arms and hands for an instant. Jonathon's joke, as he took the time to loop the rope around his wrists. Then, with a sudden powerful jerk, the noose brutally tightened before Knobby could get his fingers under the taut rope. Thus began the strangulation and ultimate death of Knobby Gault, private investigator. Jonathon's arms flexed and, with the rope looped around his hands and wrists, he continued toward the deadly eventual fate of his victim. Knobby's legs flailed out in a wild, crazy dance while his hands unsuccessfully tore at his throat. The whites of his eyes bulged and grew bloody. Blood seeped under the skin above and below his eyes. The heels of his shoes beat scrapes and scuffmarks on the polished wood floor. Ugly, gurgling sounds eventually diminished as his efforts dimmed and his final attempts to twist and turn away from his attacker failed.

Jonathon, now in a heavy sweat, giggled and applied additional backpressure on the rope, testing for further resistance from Knobby. There was none. Finally crossing his hands and delivering the *coup de grâce*, he then released his death grip on the now dead Knobby Gault.

"Well now, that was fun. Michael, come look at the disrespectful, bad man now," said Jonathon, his eyes blazing with excitement. Michael approached and with a frown looked away from the dead man whose face was a grotesque mask of pain.

"We must load him into the boot of the Bentley, and dispose of him tonight," was Jonathon's final order of the evening as he returned the coiled rope to his pocket. This day had been most productive: loose ends all neatly tied up.

CHAPTER 14

Trevor waited for his friend, Chief Inspector Albert LaGrange, outside the New Scotland Yard building at Number 10 Broadway, SW1 in London. When LaGrange emerged from the stainless steel building, he approached and greeted him with,

"Good morning Trev, and how you are today?"

"Feeling pretty good now that we can get to Knobby and his so-called alibi witness today."

LaGrange led him to the police van and opened the rear door for Trevor while he got in the front passenger seat. A Metropolitan police constable drove the duo to the last known address of Knobby Gault to interview him again in hopes of obtaining additional information concerning his movements on the night of the murder of Mick Andrews.

The police car finally stopped at Knobby's address. It was a two-story residential house in the East End. All the buildings down the street looked as if made with a cookie-cutter: all drab and in mediocre condition. LaGrange knocked on the front door, which opened to reveal an old, haggard-haired, overweight woman in dull day clothes holding a worn out floor-mop.

Showing his police ID, LaGrange said, "Good morning, mum. We would like to speak to Knobby Gault. Is he in?"

"Oi 'aven't seen Knobby in a few days now. Don't know where 'e disappeared to neither. And his clothes are still 'ere."

"And his roommate, Willie Norgate: is he in today?"

"'Ere now, he's a strange one. He left 'ere bag and baggage two days ago, an' without paying me the rent money, 'e did. I 'ope you catch 'im so oi can get paid."

"Did he leave any forwarding address or phone number?""Not a peep out 'im. He's a weird one, that one is."

"Here's my card. If you hear from or remember anything about those two, please call me, day or night," said LaGrange.

"Cor Blimey, 'ave them two got in trouble?"

"We're not sure, that's why we'd like to talk to them as soon as possible."

"Aye, Oi'll call you if oi 'ear anything, for sure."

"Thank you, ma'am, and good day to you." LaGrange and Trevor looked at each other knowing they had drawn a blank for this morning's work.

"It's okay, Trevor, we'll track them down in a few days for sure," LaGrange consoled as they headed for the patrol car. "I'll have their pictures in every police vehicle throughout the kingdom. We'll get them for questioning, no doubt."

"Look here, Albert: Knobby and Willie both worked for the Johnson warehouse; both disappeared after Mick's death. Now, doesn't that tell you something isn't quite right, eh?"

"I know what you're getting at, Trevor, but it doesn't prove anything. Let's at least put them under a strong light for interrogation, then— . . . well, we'll see."

What LaGrange and Trevor did not know was that Knobby Gault was living with the fish at the bottom of the Thames River, properly anchored, never to be seen again. His mate, Willie Norgate, the lead Johnson warehouseman, had boarded the ferry in Dover and, upon his arrival in France, had disappeared without a trace.

CHAPTER 15

By the end of the following week, without receiving any police news of the disappearing duo, Trevor called a meeting that included himself, Sal Chapman, Mary Avery, and Roger, the bit-player who had run down the restaurant stairs looking for the ring. They all met at the Red Lion pub behind the New Scotland Yard building on Bedford Road. These four souls had been part of the group that many years ago had played *find the toy ring* at the Senior Johnson estate in southwest London.

The meeting at the Red Lion, held during slack business hours for partial privacy, enabled the four participants to exchange notes and to reach a consensus on the facts. The air in the room had that heavy beer scent and residue of tobacco products that befitted the ambiance of an ideal English pub.

The small group sat on low wooden stools around the equally low, dark wooden table. Daylight filtered through five stained-glass windows as a lonely pair of teenagers threw darts at a mounted dartboard, attacking the double or triple twenty. Trevor, Sal, and Roger had half-pints of beer, while Mary was quite content nursing a gin and tonic.

Trevor leaned forward and said, "All right, fellow confidants, let's see what we have so far. Mary, you first: has Jonathon showed you the ring yet?"

"Yes, he has, and I certainly played up how expensive it looked. With fifty-six cut and polished facets, it definitely fits the part!"

"So, he has not had it appraised as yet?"

"I don't think so, Trevor; he seems to take pleasure in just ownership right now. I'm sure he keeps it locked in his desk in that big library room of his."

"Oh, Mary, good timing in letting Sal know when Jonathon was coming down that staircase in the restaurant. Same for you Roger, good work there. Jonathon certainly fell for the trap. Okay, now Sal: have there been any additional developments with you since you took care of Jonathon's unsuccessful punch-up some weeks ago?"

"No, I daresay he learned a lesson in that regard from that night's thrashing of his two Foundry blokes. Ai, that Jonathon is a slippery, clever one, he is."

"Much too clever I'm afraid." Trevor looked at each of his friends and then with his head bowed said, "I'm at the point of dissolving this sting operation of mine to catch Jonathon in a petty theft." He took a deep breath and continued, "Elizabeth made me realize that my obsession for revenge has caused a great deal of harm to me personally and to our marriage. I just cannot go on with this scheme." Looking up he continued, "I am sorry for bringing you all into my childish plan. I do appreciate all your time and work you have dedicated. I'm not too pleased with myself, and I intend to confess and call off this conspiracy . . . *to Jonathon in person.*"

Trevor waited for remarks from his friends. However, they all shrugged their shoulders, and admitted that it was, at least, worth a try.

"Too bad. That Jonathon needs punishment for sure," said Sal.

"Unfortunately, that's not for me to decide or administer." Trevor stood up and faced his friends, "Right now, I feel partially responsible for Mick Andrews' death. In addition to everything else, I'll have to deal with my guilt in that regard. Thank you again, and feel free to carry on with your own life's tribulations. May they all be minor ones."

After Trevor paid the bill and left, the trio remained in the pub to finish their drinks.

"Really, I could completely understand Trevor's psychological reasoning to get back at Jonathon. That beating, *and for nothing*, must have been a terrible burden for a young boy to absorb and live with for all those years. It was so brutally unfair and uncalled for." All echoed Mary's conclusion.

CHAPTER 16

"Sir Jonathon, there is a gentleman at the door whose name is Trevor Zelcorr II." Michael read from the business card in his hand.

"Trevor Zelcorr, you say?" Jonathon, seated at his desk, was fully dressed and wearing a smoking jacket with an expensive fur collar that extended down the front to near his belt line. His vast desk occupied the space in front of a large, semi-shaded window. He looked up, removed his glasses and remarked, "Trevor Zelcorr indeed." Jonathon sucked up another line of cocaine into his nose. The powder came off the glass plate that rested on his desk. He leaned back and insured the drug would be completely absorbed into his system with an extra influx of air. He replaced the plate into a bottom drawer of the massive desk, coughed once, shook his head, and smoothed back his mop of slightly graying hair.

"Show the gentleman in, Michael; this could be rather interesting."

After all these years, what does that weakling want? A political favor? Possibly a donation to some worthless cause or other? However, he will get nothing from me. Absolutely nothing!

Michael entered the room and held the door open for Trevor to proceed. He did and stopped momentarily to observe the large library room. When he saw Jonathon at his desk, Trevor approached and stood approximately a dozen feet from the man he had come to see. Meanwhile, Michael detoured to his assigned area near the bar, in partial shadow, and kept his vigilant position. Jonathon got up and placed himself half-seated at the front of his desk, arms folded.

"Well, well, look at sickly little Trevor Zelcorr all grown up and possibly scratching for a favor, eh?"

"I didn't come here to insult, or fight with you, Jonathon, and a matter of—"

"That's *Sir Jonathon* to you, you miserable, half-wit barrister!" Jonathon stood erect, fists at his sides, his chin thrust out, glaring at Trevor.

"And it's *Zelcorr the Second* to you, *sir*."

"Touché," acknowledged Jonathon with a forced smile, raising an eyebrow and cocking his head. "'One for the Gipper' as they say in America. Now, what is it you want?"

"Before you interrupted me, I was trying to say that I've come here to apologize, and to confess my plan to bait you into committing a petty crime so that I could bring a criminal complaint against you. Rather a payback for the beating you inflicted upon me years ago. However, I've just dismantled my scheme players, and do hereby state that I am sorry, and do hope you accept my apology."

The unexpected confession took Jonathon by surprise. He folded his arms again, leaned back onto his desk, and faced Trevor. "I dare say, now you have me curious to learn what sort of plan or scheme you had in mind. Pray do continue, Trevor."

"The ring, Jonathon, the diamond ring you took from the Yorkshire Arms Gents room. I relied on your greed to acquire possessions—a well-known gossip subject in most circles of the community—and you fell for the bait."

"The ring? I found an abandoned ring, and acquired it, so what, mister junior detective?" Jonathon's insides began to simmer, his nerve pulses activated into hyper-mode.

"That ring you so-called *acquired* is, in fact, a fake, an imitation diamond made of glass, total value, perhaps fifty pounds, most of it for the workmanship. You would have known that from an appraisal by any proficient jeweler."

Jonathon instantly bolted upright.

"WHAT?— *YOU . . . FAKE . . .*?" His eyes bulged, his arms flailed, his breathing rasped as he rounded his desk, fumbled with some keys and yanked opened a drawer. He withdrew the ring, rushed to a window, and threw a heavy curtain aside for a closer inspection.

"Yes, look closely at that imitation, Jonathon. It fits you perfectly. Notice the facet cuts are not that sharp. . . Any expert jeweler could have confirmed its value. That is the truth, the whole truth. I do hope you accept my apology."

Jonathon lowered his hand, turned and faced Trevor.

"Accept your apology?" His voice rose a good octave, his eyes blazed, his insides burned. He now screamed, "Here's my answer, you six-pence, underhanded, impudent bastard. Here, take back your phony jewelry!" as he hurled the ring straight at Trevor, who caught it. "Now you are in possession of the stolen ring. It is yours, which clears me of your stupid plan. Michael, come here and teach this disrespectful, arrogant puppy not to play in the big league." Jonathon's eyes flashed with a glee of anticipation.

Michael stepped out from the shadows and slowly put himself between Trevor and his employer. He faced Trevor, who by now had removed his suit jacket and laid it on a near-by club chair. In a display of superior confidence, Michael flexed his muscles, leisurely rotated his head, and cracked his knuckles. *Not a good sign*, thought Trevor as he prepared for the ensuing punch-up. A sinister giggle from Jonathon, now behind his desk, assured his attendance to witness the demise of Trevor Zelcorr II.

Michael executed a surprisingly fast and athletic three-step advance, followed by a flying sidekick, without a flaw. However, Trevor quickly recognized the attack, parried the air-borne foot with his right hand, and sent Michael unceremoniously to the floor, Wrumph! *Damn, I hate to fight an old man.* Trevor disliked the position he had put himself in, now forced to fight.

With the agility of a young leopard, Michael sprang to his feet. The two men circled each other, arms *en garde*, fists clenched; their faces showed the seriousness of the situation. Both fighters threw punches and kicks, and both blocked them. Trevor had the edge in speed, but Michael possessed the knowledge from extensive experience and connected with a punch that sent Trevor reeling. Another punch propelled him over one of the club chairs. Nevertheless, with a low spinning back-kick, Trevor catapulted Michael airborne again to meet the floor once more. The two men exchanged grunts and groans, but not a single comprehensible word. Michael, now nearing the bar, picked up one of several barstools and advanced his attack. Trevor, seeing it coming, ducked under a wild horizontal swing. He quickly rose up and punched the backside of Michael's arm just above the elbow. The resulting stinger caused Michael to drop his now useless arm. He tried to raise the stool with his other hand, but Trevor connected a solid left hook that sent Michael sprawling into one of the rolling wooden ladders. Before he could fully recover, Trevor landed a hard right cross to Michael's temple; he slumped to the floor again, this time out cold.

"*Bloody hell*! So you've been working out, I see. No more skinny, weakling kid, eh?" Jonathon rounded the desk and confronted Trevor. He released the two-foot length of rope from his pocket and casually swung it *tick-tock* in front of his leg. Cocaine residue was clearly visible around his nostrils as his drug- and alcohol-stimulated body began a slow transformation, his menacing eyes wide open, his face a mask of hate and vengeance.

"I've beaten you down a long time ago, Trevor, and now I'll do it again. You will receive the same ultimate punishment as all those who insult, defy, and plot against me. Yes, my dear Trevor, like those recent two dumb amateurs who once worked for you. What were their names? Oh yes, Mick Andrews and Knobby Gault. Really, Trevor, you should have hired more qualified professionals."

"What do you mean, **once** worked for me?" Trevor doubled his fists. With anger and revulsion heating up his insides, he advanced toward Jonathon. But with a fast slap of Jonathon's rope, a red bruise quickly registered on Trevor's cheek. He touched his face, then stepped back, tore off his necktie and wrapped the small end around his hand. As the two men circled each other, Trevor snapped out his only weapon and marked a small sting at the corner of Jonathon's eye.

Unfazed and feeling no pain, Jonathon confessed in a most assured manner, "You will pay for that snip. You see, Trevor, I sent both of your meddling investigators to the bottom of the Thames, to be sure."

"YOU . . .! *YOU* . . . responsible for their deaths?"

"Most certainly, my dear Trevor. No one gets in my way, or interferes with my business. That Mick investigator of yours got too nosey into my warehouse affairs, and that Knobby bloke failed to properly execute my orders for Mick's demise."

Jonathon stepped around Trevor with the bravado of assumed confidence. "And if you think that my confession to you would jeopardize my freedom, think again, you stupid moron. If you believe I would be brainless enough to endanger my position with a confession, then you, dear Trevor, are most emphatically mistaken, for you will not leave this room alive."

"You filthy, murderous, homicidal swine! I hope you rot in hell for eternity." Trevor, shaken and horrified at Jonathon's declaration of guilt, hoped it was enough for him to hang for his crimes. He truly hated the monster in front of him.

"Oh, look what I found," gestured Jonathon as he removed the small voice recorder from his trousers. "Do you know what it is? No? Well then, let me tell you."

Jonathon turned the small device over repeatedly in his hand, frequently glancing at Trevor to monitor his reaction. "This voice recorder was removed from Mick Andrews' pocket before his visit to the river. Be advised that the data within has been deleted and swept clean. Oops—oh look! I've dropped it," he mocked as it fell to the floor. Without another word, Jonathon repeatedly stomped on the device until it splintered and shattered into several pieces. "You can have that along with your phony ring." With a sweep of his foot, Jonathon sent some broken parts skidding along the polished floor. He then threw back his head and shrieked like a *banshee*.

Trevor could no longer contain his rage as he charged into Jonathon, finishing with a flying punch that propelled Jonathon head over heels.

Insanity lurked within those bloodshot, drug-polluted eyes, in that body erupting into violence. However, with surprising agility Jonathon bounced up, and with vile multiple curses and blood streaming from his nose, he charged at Trevor. With a smooth double-wave of his hands and a slight pressure on Jonathon's arm, Trevor sent his attacker to the floor once again. *Thank you, Tai Chi.*

When Jonathon regained his weakened stance, Trevor closed in with a straight punch to his face.

"I retract my apology," he growled as he smashed his fist into Jonathon's face again. "That one was for Mick Andrews." Trevor pulled Jonathon up by his furry lapel, and with another blow, he hit him again in the same spot. "And that was a long time coming. I'm through with you, Jonathon, you filthy pig. You are a disgrace to the government and to all people in the UK—*and* to all humanity, for that matter."

"Ha . . . ha . . .! You . . . think . . . you've . . . won? Well, you have . . . nothing . . . no . . . proof . . . *nothing!*" The words sounded hollow as once again Jonathon, showing discoloration and swelling from the battle, regained his shaky, wide-stance footing.

Trevor went to check on Michael who proved to still be in never-never land. Jonathon, holding a bloody handkerchief to his face, slowly inched his way toward the library double doors.

"Before you try to leave Jonathon, I have something to show *you.*" Trevor reached into his pocket, and then held up a small digital audio recorder. Holding it high, "It's all here, you sick bastard, all in your own words: a full confession to the murders of Mick and Knobby. *Who is the half-wit now?*"

The image of young Jonathon holding a colorful toy ring high over his head, flashed for an instant then dissipated forever from Trevor's psyche. He was free at last.

"NOOO-O O!" Jonathon screamed as he retreated to flee the room. He threw both doors open only to be confronted by Chief Inspector Albert LaGrange and four of London's finest Metropolitan Policemen.

LaGrange entered, stepped aside and motioned his officers to restrain Jonathon.

"NO, you . . . can't— don't . . . touch me! I have an *OBE*. You will . . . be . . . reprimanded . . . severely. LET ME GO!"

"Inspector LaGrange, would you kindly detain Sir Jonathon Malcolm Johnson for the murder of Mick Andrews and one named Knobby Gault. Also, if you wake up his butler, arrest him as an accomplice. He would probably plea for a reduced sentence while in custody," said Trevor.

Two police officers revived Michael, handcuffed him and led him out. The other two officers struggling with Jonathon finally subdued him and led the deranged man out to a police van. He was still screaming curses and objections, and attempting to intimidate through his connections to influential politicians.

LaGrange looked at Trevor and remarked, "You don't look like the champion, but you certainly won the fight." Trevor managed a smile through a swollen lip and handed the voice recorder to the chief inspector.

"Here it is, Albert. It has all the evidence you'll need."

"Well now, it looks like Sir Jonathon cracked from discovering he pinched a fake diamond ring. We heard most of that through the door." LaGrange continued, "Strange how greed can cause some people to lose their sense of common decency. We lucked out here today, Trevor, ol' boy. Funny thing: your aborted sting unexpectedly produced results in bringing our murder case to resolution. I thank you, Trevor."

"And thank you for suggesting your backup plan for my coming here. I hadn't expected any of this happening; although I must say Jonathon's violent temper is legendary." After they shook hands, the two friends left the library and LaGrange headed for his police van.

Waiting in the hallway, Elizabeth stepped forward and greeted her husband with a loving embrace. She took a step back and said, "Oh dear, look at you. Now you promised me that you wouldn't fight."

"Well, just a little—mostly self defense, I think." Trevor smiled and held her in his arms.

"Chief Inspector LaGrange was right, Trev, you look a mess, but I do love you so very much."

"Here now, I could do with a bath and a good deal of tender loving care, woman. Will you join me?"

"I most certainly will. Let's go home, Trev. Please hurry."

The End

M.L. Barbani

EPILOGUE

Jonathon Malcolm Johnson and Michael Harrington were tried for the murders of Mick Andrews and Knobby Gault. The verdict handed down: Guilty. Both men received long prison sentences along with additional jail time for operating a massive illicit drug operation.

In time, the prison psychiatrist declared Jonathon insane, and had him transferred to a mental institution. He remained there under lock and key for the remainder of his prison term.

The Metropolitan Police Narcotics Team searched the Johnson warehouse, from which they removed approximately two tons of illegal narcotics. The haul was transported to an incinerator facility outside of London where, under the watchful eyes of two police officers, the drug bundles were reduced to ashes.

At the estate of Jonathon Malcolm Johnson, another search team discovered a small locked closet stacked with *'pictures of the queen'*: GBP currency worth over six million pounds.

For his role in the apprehension of the criminals, the drug discovery, and the enormous retrieval of currency from the Johnson estate, Chief Inspector Albert LaGrange now enjoyed the promotion to Superintendent, Metropolitan Police- London.

Elizabeth and Trevor Zelcorr II, celebrated the joyous news of her pregnancy while they vacationed on the Isle of Capri, Italy.

M.L. Barbani

The Candlelight
Conspiracy

DEDICATION

To Warren Publishing, Inc.—Cathy Brophy, President; Jere Armen, editor; and staff—for getting my work to be interesting and readable. It was your work that made it all happen. Thank you.

To my old friend and past co-worker, Daniel Para, who lives in Northern Spain. I am grateful for his command of both English and Spanish languages. He guided me as well through the complex spelling of the Basque language which, in fact, has no known origin. I thank you, Dan, for your tireless support and patience.

Also, to all members of the Pamlico Writers Group in Washington, North Carolina, for their critiques of my writing. Members include poets, fiction, and historical writers as: Nancy Clark, Angela Silverthorne, Jerry Cuthrell, Ralph Dramstad, Donna Lay, Ann Meyers, Joseph Haranzo, Jim Keen, Lane Schroeder, Doris Schneider, Ken Schwenk, Natasha Roberson, Herta Abarr, James Lupton, and many others.

I thank you all, present and past members.

If we have not peace
within ourselves,
it is in vain
to seek it
from outward sources.

— Francois de La Rochefoucauld

FORWARD

FACT... The Basque people have lived in the northern part of Spain in the provinces of Vizcaya, Guipúzcoa, Alava, Navarra, and in the French region of Pyrénees-Atlantique since well before Roman times.

Euskadi Ta Askatasuna (ETA) in the Basque language translates as "Basque country and liberty." ETA is a Basque paramilitary group that seeks to create an independent socialist state for the Basque people, separate from Spain and France. ETA, the terrorist arm of the Basque movement, was founded in 1959, and its deadly objective of kidnapping and murder continues to this day.

PROLOGUE

El País, Spain's newspaper, reports:

April 25, 1986

In Madrid, at the corner of Principe de Vergara and Juan Bravo Streets, a car bomb activated by remote control exploded as a Guardia Civil Land Rover drove by. The five officers inside the vehicle were killed and four nearby civilian shoppers also died; three were Americans, and one was a young Spanish hiker. The continuing terror attacks by ETA sparked national outrage and brought an estimated six million Spaniards onto the bloody streets of the country in protests. Investigations persist, and the struggle for a political solution continues.

CHAPTER 1

Michael Lamont Keller is a pretty good engineer. Oh, he is no Albert Einstein, but a well above average engineer in his chosen field. Thirty-four years old and five-ten in height, he fits the mold of your typical Electronics/Communications Engineer. Heck, even his weight and physical appearance went along with the flock of stamped out graduates from many of the universities that occupied the eastern part of America. Mike graduated in 1986, then spent two years fulfilling his military duty overseas. He was selected and attached to several United Nations forensic experts in examining bodies found among mass graves in the Balkan province of Kosovo. Identification and mode of death would be recorded when possible. It was quite a change from Mike's college education, but the work kept him in excellent physical condition.

After his tour and honorable discharge, General Products Incorporated of Owings Mills, Maryland, recruited him as a Member of the Technical Staff. He then worked his way up to Senior Project Engineer. Mike has thick brown hair, hazel eyes, a ruddy complexion, and is built like a brick outhouse. He has a nice face and, with no redeeming features, is easily missed in a crowd. Hunting and fishing are his hobbies. Nothing special, just an outdoor guy with a love of nature and keeping fit to enjoy it all.

His parents are both college graduates with master's degrees in their fields of expertise. Mother's degree was in English, and his father graduated with a command of electronics and computer science. With a little persuasion, Michael Lamont Keller followed their example when it came to education. Elena Salazar, Mike's grandmother, was also a graduate student with a master's degree in Romance languages.

Now comfortably married to his college sweetheart, Mike has the American dream by the tail on a down-hill drag. Oh, he loves his wife Beebe, but they're still without children. So, Mike spends some of his spare time hunting and fishing with a small group of male friends. And, twice a week, he attends and works out with Kim Yoshiro Whang who holds a Fifth Degree Black Belt in Korean Taekwondo. In this field of martial arts, Mike has mastered the brown belt degree and is working on his black belt level with success. He also taught Beebe many self-defense moves in the event she is attacked. *Lord, I hope that never happens,* was Mike's concern. She socializes with several wives of the engineers and joins her husband in a local shooting club. Life is indeed good to the young married couple.

Little did Mike realize that this day, the nineteenth of February, 2006, would change his life forever.

CHAPTER 2

Mike Keller was at his desk in rolled up shirt sleeves studying a section of schedules from one of the many government projects the company was involved in, completing an on-time-under-budget time-table. It was ten in the morning, with a howling wind outside his window promising rain to follow, making it a truly miserable day—thank God it was outside. However, an invisible, separate thunder and lightning storm was brewing within the corporate hierarchy.

Ron Lecrox, a lead supervisor, stepped into Mike's office, maneuvered behind Mike, and tapped him on the shoulder.

"Whoa, don't scare me like that!" Mike spun his leather padded chair around to face him.

"Sorry about that Mike, but I, uh . . . do have some nasty news. And damn it, I was elected to transmit the order."

"Well, let me guess, you can't make it this weekend for the turkey hunt. Or, you want *my* wife to run away with you to Tahiti." Mike smiled and waved him to a chair. Ron sat down and lowered his voice.

"All kidding aside, Mike, the boss confessed that the company is downsizing, and a lot of positions and projects will be terminated."

"Ah yes, the good old RIF (Reduction in Force). I heard something about that a couple weeks ago. Hey, Ron, don't tell me you're on that list."

"No, Mike, not me . . . but you are. Hey, I double-checked to be damn sure. This is no joke."

Mike stiffened in his chair as if a cold stab had struck him in the pit of his stomach. With blank eyes, he looked at his friend, hoping he had misunderstood what he just heard. He put his hands together as if in silent prayer while tapping his nose several times.

"Mike, we all know you're a good engineer, so why do they always start cutting from the top?" Mike raised his hand and cut off Ron's speech. With his hands clasped again, he slowly turned, placed his elbows on the desk with his forehead resting on his fingertips, his eyes closed.

"I am really sorry to bring you this lousy news," Ron concluded.

"Please leave now." Mike's voice was low and almost inaudible. Ron did not hesitate and retreated from the office. When Mike turned around, his office walls seemed to spin as he tried to focus on all the Good ol' Boy awards his short career had amassed. *Big freakin' deal, and now I'm without a job. Geeze, how am I going to break this to Beebe? Her plans for the house . . .* Mike's office began to spin again. *Get a grip!*

Taking a deep breath, he straightened up and decided to see the official notice in the Administration Office. Mike rolled down his sleeves and snatched his jacket off a plastic hanger. He then took one of the hall elevators to the main floor, crossed over to the east end of the marble and glass building, and entered the Admin office. Judy Parker, at her desk, started to smile when she saw Mike, but suppressed it, fully suspecting why he had arrived.

"Hello, Mike."

"Hi, Judy. I uh, suppose you may know why I'm here this lousy morning?"

"Well, from your tone, I'll guess it's about the notice. I was going to bring the official order up to you when I was told that the termination would take place with your section personnel. I'm so sorry to have to see you leave. The company cut several projects. Unfortunately, yours was one of them. Mike, you were *not* at fault in any regard." She paused, looked uncomfortable and finally added, "Anyway, I'll have all the necessary forms for you to sign, but there's no hurry." She handed him the official notice of termination.

"Six years down the drain." Mike spoke on a sour note, turned away from the secretary, and stuffed the notice into his jacket pocket. A few dazed steps took him to a bulletin board where he placed his hand on the wall to steady himself. There, several announcements were posted. Without intent or purpose, he scanned the notices when he stopped at a line that read:

Opening: Senior Project Engineer for posting at our new facility in Madrid, Spain. Degree, five years experience in project management, secrecy clearance, ability to speak and write Spanish fluently are required. No exceptions.

Contact: Sandi Montoya Dennison, room 104.

I can do this, Mike's insides shouted. *God bless Grandma Elena for insisting that Mom and Dad make sure I be educated in dual languages. Muchas gracias, abuela—may you rest in peace. Now, hang on to your shorts, Sandi, here I come!*

CHAPTER 3

The interview with Sandi Dennison went without a single flaw. Sandi recommended Michael Keller for the assignment to Spain, as *highly qualified*. His paperwork was transmitted up to the division chief, where Samuel Richards would review the documents and, if he signed off, would present them to the company president for the final approval.

* * * * *

It was toward the end of this eventful day that Mike Keller met with the company president and CEO, Charles W. Brandson. He was a huge, well-built man in his mid-fifties with brown eyes that did not match his emerging peek-a-boo gray hair. On his way up the company ladder, Charles Brandson broke many a man both physically and intellectually to finally take charge of the company.

Mike sat erect and confident in an overstuffed leather chair in front of the president's massive desk. As Brandson leafed through the assorted papers in Mike's file, he noted, "I see that you've scored a perfect twenty—speak and write—on the language test. Good for you."

He continued alternating between the file papers and glancing at Mike. Charles finally checked some last pages, closed the file, and directed his full attention to the man sitting in front of him.

"Michael, I'm terribly sorry to have cancelled the project you were working on. However, it may have turned out to your advantage. Tell me, are you fully satisfied with the package Ms. Dennison explained to you? That is, the per diem, salary, storage, housing, company car, etc., etc.?"

"Yes, sir. It is most satisfactory, and I can promise you, if selected, that I'll devote one hundred and one percent of my time and talent to the Spanish project."

"Good man, because I'm going to ask the applicant to wear a couple important hats while employed out there. The facility is just north of Madrid—in the Colmenar area. It's a new eight-story building, and I'll need a sharp eye out for any abnormalities that may exist. I don't want any potential problems to develop. A great financial contract is riding on my shoulders for this Spanish project to succeed." Brandson tapped on Mike's file. "Your record here is quite impressive, and I'll be entrusting the chosen one to be my eyes and ears while on the job out there. I'll be promoting him, as Senior Project Supervisor. Well now, Michael Lamont Keller, are you with me?"

"All the way, Mister Brandson."

"Good. I'm signing your transfer and agreement. Will three weeks get you packed up and ready for your reassignment?"

"Yes sir, absolutely—no problem."

"That's what I want to hear." Charles H. Brandson stood up, stuck out a big hand that matched the rest of Charles Brandson's physique. Michael Lamont Keller shook it with smiles and vigor.

CHAPTER 4

Later that same afternoon, Mike parked his car in the garage of his home and entered through the connecting side door.

"Beebe, I'm home." Beebe emerged from the kitchen holding two cold martinis, one of the few hard drinks they occasionally indulged in.

"Hello there, mister wage earner, here's your reward for today's toil." Beebe's smile turned into a frown as she noted Mike's gloomy expression. "All right Mike, who screwed up at work today?"

Taking a deep breath, Mike took a sip of his drink, and confessed, "I'm afraid—I did, honey." He gave a deep disconcerted sigh, and sat down. "My project and my position have been eliminated—I've lost my job baby."

"*WHAT?*" Beebe put down her drink, placed one hand to her mouth, and the other onto the counter-top for support.

"But wait, we can still celebrate," added Mike.

"What in the world are you talking about? Have you gone loony? What's there to celebrate?"

Mike stood up, spread his arms out and practically shouted, "We — are — going — to — *Spain*. I got a promotion and a transfer to a fantastic project, and we'll be gone for at least a couple years or more. How about them apples!"

Beebe jumped onto Mike, her arms and legs engulfing him. She couldn't speak as he held her tight. A few tears of joy streamed down her face as she finally found her voice.

"Oh, you marvelous man, you. I'm the luckiest woman in the whole damn world!"

"I'll drink to that," and they both downed the cocktails and refilled their glasses. Beebe, five-foot-four, blond, blue-eyed, with a knock-out figure, was Mike's soul-mate for life. He fell for her the moment he first saw her. *Is it possible? Love at first sight?* Mike always thought that was a silly and childish expression until it smacked him right between the eyes . . . and loins.

"Oh my, we'll have a million things to do." Beebe turned around in small circles.

"Hey, hey, slow down, we have three weeks to pack, store up, and settle any problems that might come up. Don't worry. It'll be fine."

"Yes, of course, you're right. Let me get dinner on the table while you wash up. Go, go, go." Beebe set herself about her kitchen in a state of ecstasy and giddiness while singing whatever Spanish songs she could think of, even one called La Cucaracha—but wait, that may be a Mexican song. *Whatever! I'm happy.* With the table finally set and dinner onboard, Beebe went to the foot of the stairs and called up, "Dinner's ready, darling—oh, and by the way, tonight is definitely your lucky night."

"Yahoo!" The reply echoed down the stairs, loud and clear.

CHAPTER 5

The 747 banked slightly, then descended down smoothly from a clear blue sky onto Barajas International Airport just outside of Madrid, Spain. With baggage claimed, passports checked, and cleared through customs, Mike and Beebe then made their way through the throng of passengers and people waiting to greet their returning loved ones. Outside the great hall, a Spanish gentleman among the crowd held up a sign with the Kellers' names in full print. Below that, **General Products (ESP)** filled out the message board. After introductions were completed, the driver, Ramón Fuentes, led Mike and Beebe through the waiting crowd, then outside to a company SUV. They all piled in for the ride to their new home. Ramón explained that their shipment of household goods had already arrived and was presently located in the selected residence. Their new home was located in the Mirasierra housing district just north of the city. All the twenty-some-odd homes in that complex were almost identical in size and shape, all having a surrounding stone wall with a locked iron gate entrance. They were reportedly built by the prisoners of the Spanish Civil War under Generalísimo Franco's rule. Mike and Beebe were absolutely thrilled with their two-story, three bedroom, partially furnished interior, including front and rear patio—a true Spanish-style American home. Their neighbors would include expatriates from Europe, Asia, and other Americans. The Kellers were overjoyed to live in an international community. Life couldn't get any better. Or so it seemed. . .

CHAPTER 6

After the first few days of getting acquainted with their home and surroundings, Mike reported to work at the General Products building, which was only a few minutes' drive from his house. His first priority was for a total inspection of the new building. Although he was not classified as an executive, Mike used an unrestricted free hand—as urged by Charles W. Brandson—to examine all aspects of the building, its weaknesses and safety features.

Upon his visits to observe various laboratories, he noticed a continuous pattern of possible corporate safety violations. He arranged a tour meeting with the Spanish head of the new building, Señor José Mateo Zaragoza, who insisted on a friendly, first-name basis relationship. Spain had certainly advanced in the twentieth century.

In one particular lab, several engineers were working on interrelated components for a specific project. Test equipment, cables, and a host of other larger electronic equipment bays were located along the walls, and interspaced within the room.

"Look here, José," Mike pointed out. "I would like to see a ten-centimeter-wide, yellow caution-tape glued down around all this test equipment. If someone should accidently bump into a probe on any equipment, well, it could cause damage to the equipment and/or to the personnel involved. Don't you agree?"

"*Sí, sí,* yes, I understand what you mean." José nodded his agreement.

"The yellow floor tape should be installed in all the equipment labs that involve the electronic bays and other installed gear. It's a safety concern." Mike finished making his observation.

"I will arrange for tape purchase immediately," said José.

Mike was satisfied to learn that all the Spanish personnel employed at this facility spoke English well enough to be understood by all at General Products, ESP.

CHAPTER 7

By the end of his second work-week, Mike had completed his rounds of unofficial inspections of the building—except for the basement. After catching up with his own project assignment, Mike decided to take on that neglected area one late afternoon.

After exiting the elevator, Mike noted that the basement hallway area had a dreary appearance compared to the rest of this fairly new building. He suspected that the exposed overhead pipes, the full cable trays mounted high near the ceilings, and the dim lighting contributed to the eerie and drab atmosphere. After passing through a set of double doors, he noted that the subterranean hallway took on a more finished look, as if it had been recently reworked. Even the air seemed to have a clean but antiseptic scent. Continuing, he arrived at several large windows along his right side with drop-down black curtains on the inside that obscured any view to all passing by. The sign on the entrance door, printed in bold letters, warned:

<u>TOP SECRET CLEARANCE REQUIRED</u>
AUTHORIZED PERSONNEL ONLY
<u>NO ENTRADA SIN PERMISO</u>

Subconsciously, Mike tried the door handle and, to his surprise, it opened. He stepped into a large, brightly lit room that housed electronic racks, computers, and test equipment bays along all the walls. Some of the equipment units were new and looked like they had come out of a space-age magazine. The slight hums from the cooling fans within the bays were the only audible sounds. Behind some racks hung approximately a dozen decontamination suits, fully insulated—head to toe. Behind the decon suits was a room that looked like a chemistry lab out of a Doctor Jekyll and Mister Hyde movie, only more modern. A single word identified the room as CONTROL. Several small windows afforded a view into that room from the main electronic equipment lab. Mike tried the Control room door, but it was locked.

He turned around and centered his attention on the middle of the main floor space.

What the hell is all this? He asked himself. On top of a polished stainless steel square table rested a single, heavy, clear glass dome approximately twelve or fourteen inches high and about six to eight inches in diameter. At the top, and off to the sides, two connectors with cables were attached to the dome. One cable led down under the table to a black metal box that supplied AC power from a floor outlet nearby. The other heavier cable led down a hole in the floor—destination unknown. Mike leaned closer to the glass dome and noted a slight undulating slow motion of what looked like a heavy, pink, fluid mass. Mike murmured again, "What the—", but was interrupted with the opening of the main entrance door.

Two burly, uniformed guards with holstered nightsticks entered. With a surprised and agitated voice, one of them demanded, "Who are you and what are you doing in here?" Mike straightened up, tapped his ID badge visible on his jacket pocket, and answered, "Name here is Mike Keller. I'm the Senior Project Engineer, and I'm making an inspection tour of the building."

A guard stepped closer and challenged, "The color of your ID indicates a Secret Clearance, not TOP Secret as the door sign clearly states."

"My new clearance will take a bit more time to come through. Now, if you're so concerned, why was that door *un*locked?" countered Mike.

"We do the questioning here, wise guy." By this time, both guards were at Mike's side, gripping his arms and pointing him toward the door.

Mike gave a violent shrug that freed himself from his captors, and with sarcasm declared, "I know how to walk, and I don't need your help."

Mike knew better than to ask what was going on in this room. True, he was out of bounds here, but he figured he held the ace in the hole with the unlocked Top Secret door.

Both guards followed Mike out, with a trailing and threatening remark from one, "You'll pay for crashing this party, buddy Mike." The menacing statement came as one guard pointed his nightstick at Mike's back.

While walking toward the building exit doors, Mike raised his hand and gave them a single finger wave. He figured that the guards, Jack Rymes and Lou Martin, as indicated by their ID badges, would not push this incident too far due to their blunder in leaving that particular door unlocked. *Status quo?* Actually, there would be hell to pay.

The guards watched Mike walk back down the hallway to exit the building. One guard kept tapping his open hand with his nightstick. "Damn it, we screwed up this time."

CHAPTER 8

The cool late May night's air, along with the enjoyment of Beebe's company and cocktails, could not lift Mike's feeling of anxiety and discomfiture. They sat outside in the rear patio of their home in this foreign land that echoed the good life back stateside. Mike rarely discussed his work with his wife due to the sensitivity and classification of most projects he worked on, or managed. Beebe sensed his rather quiet and uneasy mood this evening after his return from Colmenar.

"Just look at those beautiful clear stars." Beebe scanned the night sky with her delicate hand.

"Umm," was Mike's preoccupied answer.

"All right, Miguel," she used the Spanish term for his name, "let's have the problem of this workday."

"Oh, you are much too clever, my beautiful wife. Well, let's just say that I was caught with my hand in the proverbial cookie jar." He then pulled a good tote of his martini.

"Good Lord, don't you tell me that you stole something from the company." Beebe's tone expressed her concern.

"Oh no, *mi amor*, it's just that I goofed and I was where I should not have been; a momentary slip of the conscious mind. Relax now; I'm sure nothing will come of the incident."

"It better not, lover. Remember, tomorrow night is our anniversary and you promised me a night out." That got Mike back into a good mood.

"Right-on. Tell you what, how about having *tapas*, then dinner downtown, and finally take in a Flamenco show to wind up the evening?"

"Sounds like a good plan to me. Let's finish up here, and get a good night's sleep."

Because of his earlier confrontation with the security guards, Mike slept with some apprehension that night. Furthermore, he dreamed that he was climbing a vertical ladder that was supposed to change to an easier downward curve that never materialized. Worse yet, his desperate haste to get away from a menacing, gelatinous, blob that might soon overtake him loomed ever so close.

CHAPTER 9

The next work day proved to be an uneventful one. No word came down about the Top Secret room. Mike felt at ease for the rest of the morning. Yesterday's goof could have been a nasty blemish, and an embarrassing negative report on his record. However, later in the day, Mike's name did come up to monitor an experiment for a few extra after-hours. The scheduled project engineer was unexpectedly delayed. Upon his arrival he would relieve Mike, and then the late engineer would resume his proper obligation.

Damn, Beebe will crucify me if I mess up this special night. Mike made several urgent in-house calls to find an alternate to take his place. With luck, Hilario Fuentes, a young promising Spanish engineer, volunteered to help fix Mike's overtime dilemma. Hilario, considered bright, energetic, and willing to go the extra kilometer when needed, worked in the same section as Mike.

"*Muchisimas gracias*, Hilario. I won't forget this huge favor, my friend." Indeed, Mike planed to give him a case of a most expensive vintage wine.

"*De nada, me place*; I have no plans for this evening." Hilario was eager and happy to assist the American Senior Engineer. And that entry would look good in Hilario's near-empty file folder.

Later that evening, Mike and Beebe were almost dressed for their anniversary party night out. The plan was to enjoy some *tapas*-hopping well before the dinner hour—which takes place around ten in the evening. While dressing, Mike heard their phone ring. Beebe answered it.

"Hello, yes?" A slight pause, then, "Yes, of course, *un momento, por favor.*" Putting her hand over the mouthpiece, she called out.

"Mike, it's for you—someone from the company."

"That's strange, okay, I'll take it in here."

"Hello, *sí*, this is Señor Keller speaking." Mike listened. In short order, a frown brought his eyebrows together. "Oh, no. *Dios mio*. Are you sure?" Another short pause—"*Sí, sí, sí*, yes of course—I'll be there." Mike hung up the phone and reached for his shirt and jacket.

"Did you hear?" he asked Beebe.

"You know that I don't listen in on your phone calls. So, what's happened?"

"There's been an accident at work. An engineer was found motionless at the foot of a stair-well. They think he's dead. A lot of people have been notified—the senior managers, hell, even the police. I'm awful sorry, sweetheart, but I've got to get out there and find out who, and what actually happened."

"Oh no, not tonight." Beebe put on a hurt face.

"I'll be back as soon as possible, I promise."

Beebe sighed, "I understand, of course. I'll be waiting in my new black dress."

Mike finished dressing, kissed his wife at the front door, and added, "Damn, you look dynamite tonight. I'll definitely be back quick as a wink."

Beebe listened to Mike's car rush off into the darkening night and mumbled, "Happy Anniversary, girl."

CHAPTER 10

Mike pulled up into the company's parking lot that should have been almost empty by now. However, many cars and police vans were parked near the entrance. He sprinted into the building, paused, listened, and followed the sounds of people talking just down the hallway. He ran towards the commotion and stopped at the edge of a group of employees and managers. "What happened here? Who got hurt?"

"Oh, Señor Keller, it is Hilario Fuentes, there at the bottom of the stairway. They say he is dead," someone said.

"NO, no, not Hilario—dead?" Mike made his way to the head of the stairs. Policemen were at the bottom along with a medical examiner, who was wiping his bloody hands with a small towel. He then quietly spoke to Ramón Fuentes, the father of the deceased. A policeman stopped Mike at the bottom of the stairwell, but José Zaragoza, the building manager, motioned him through with a wave of his hand. He had been talking to a policeman who was heading the investigation of the incident. José introduced Mike to the chief investigator.

"What happened here?" Mike was visibly shaken at seeing Hilario's body and the blood smears along the wall and stairs. Juan Antonio Sapporo, the policeman in charge, spoke perfect English.

"It appears, this young man may have slipped, or tripped and fell down all ten steps to the bottom, and landing, as you see, near the wall."

Ramón was almost in tears, "My son, my son." He reached for a handkerchief as Mike put a strong arm around him to console his friend.

"I'm so very sorry, Ramón. I feel partly to blame. I asked Hilario to work this evening."

Ramón brushed the apology aside with a wave of his hand, and sobbed, "How could this happen?"

Mike was no detective, although he had served as a monitor of murdered civilians during his military tour of the war in Kosovo some years ago. It was basically a body count and data recovery operation. Consequently, he had knowledge and experience of what constituted a crime scene over that from an accident.

While waiting for a stretcher to arrive and remove the body, Mike leaned down and first noted Hilario's shoes. They were a pair of running style with what looked like anti-slip soles—heel to toe. Next he studied a long U-shaped head wound hardly visible along just above his right ear. Coagulated blood almost disguised that wound. *What caused that type of injury?* he wondered.

The stretcher team arrived and pushed their way through the now diminished group of onlookers. The police ordered the people to disperse, but asked for Ramón and Mike to remain for additional questioning. Still at the bottom of the stairwell, Mike looked up as the stretcher team ascended carrying the covered body of Hilario. Just then Mike saw the two guards at the head of the stairs; one was tapping his nightstick into his open hand. For a very brief instant, he made eye contact with one of them. A shiver ran through Mike's body. The guards turned and left the area along with several remaining people. What was in that eye contact that so unnerved Mike?

The chief investigator took Mike's arm aside and asked him various questions . . . name, address, telephone number, and what information he could provide in the matter.

Ramón also was questioned and apologies were made for the delays in the interrogation. Señor Zaragoza also remained, talked to the chief, and to Mike and Ramón. No one had a positive explanation for what caused Hilario to be found dead at the bottom of the stairwell. The police were pushing the theory that he slipped or tripped and fell, ultimately hitting his head on the wall and/or steps several times before coming to rest at the bottom. Mike had a different scenario, but kept it to himself for the moment. Also, his promise to Beebe for an early return soon faded from his mind.

After several hours had passed, Mike offered to invite Ramón to a local after-hours café that remained open. Ramón talked about his son, and vouched for Hilario's willingness to help people whenever possible.

"Do you know of anyone who would want to harm him?" Mike presented this new avenue of questioning.

"No, Señor, no one. My son had no enemies—*ninguno*. Everyone always had good things to say about him."

This line of discussion produced no leads at all. After several coffees and cognacs, the two men called it a night.

"*Buenas noches, Ramón.* Take care, my friend. Please give my condolences to your wife." They both briefly embraced, then departed the café. When Mike arrived home, Beebe was still up but in her night clothes. He apologized for the late hour and gave some details of the Hilario mystery. Beebe could see how distressed Mike was and did not bring up the anniversary date. She hid her disappointment well and did not complain.

It turned out to be a long, party-ending night.

CHAPTER 11

With controlled anger building up in Charles H. Brandson's voice, he spoke harshly into the phone.

"What the hell is going on over there? And who is it that was found dead at the bottom of a stairwell?" Brandson waited for the answers provided by José Zaragoza.

"Get Michael Keller on the phone; maybe he knows something more about this." After a short pause, "Hello, Mike, do you know anything of this disturbing affair?"

"No sir, what you were told is what appears to be simply an unfortunate accident."

"Well, let's certainly keep it that way. We don't want any kind of adverse publicity floating around because of that incident. And, make sure you limit the damn news media. Do you understand me, Mike?"

"Yes, I do, Charles." However, Mike did not understand Brandon's attitude. *What was he afraid of? Bad publicity?*

The next day, it was as if the building had shut down. That is, nothing really was accomplished, as people shuffled between offices in a state of shock. The truth is that they were in a state of disbelief and sorrow. How could it be that one of their own intelligent, young, and healthy engineers could be dead from a fall within their modern building? *What a terrible accident.*

By noon, the company's head called and notified everyone that the rest of the business day had been cancelled. Thus began the remainder of the day as one of mourning for young Hilario Fuentes. His father, Ramón, had not showed up for work.

Mike returned to his home in a somber and puzzled mood. He had his own questions about last night's death scene. Why was there so much blood along the wall beginning from almost the very top of the stairs?

What caused that strange wound in Hilario's head? And, why were the two guards glaring at Mike from the top of the stairwell? *Still smarting from the unlocked secret room?*

It would take a week after the funeral service for Hilario Fuentes to be buried and laid to rest before Mike and Beebe remade their plans for a night out to celebrate their anniversary.

CHAPTER 12

"Hey, Beebe, since most of the *tapas* places are downtown in old Madrid, I figure we take a taxi down there; it should be a lot easier than me to try to find them, not including fighting the traffic. What do you say?"

"You're the boss man," replied Beebe as she stepped out of the bedroom while still putting in place that one troublesome earring.

"So, that's what that little black dress looks like," Mike said as he finished off his martini.

"I'm glad you like it; play your cards right and I'll even let you rip it off me later tonight." Even after many years of marriage, they still managed to have fun with each other. Mike and Beebe were just plain happy to be alive, working, and in good health.

The taxi ride into old Madrid was uneventful. The driver finally let them out onto a narrow street that sported several *tapas* bars. At eight PM the bars were crowded with young and old people enjoying the early night out. The Kellers immersed themselves into the atmosphere of good cheer, experiencing some new, strange, and delicious snacks. Mike had no problem with the language as he spoke and understood it perfectly. Beebe was no slouch and understood more than she spoke. When they finished, Mike paid the bill by handing some notes over the heads of patrons. The sum satisfied *la cuenta*. It was off to another *tapas* bar to sample their specialties. It was just a few doors down the street. Beebe's light sweater and Mike's suit were enough to be comfortable in the cool night air as they walked and skipped a happy beat.

At the proper time, around ten PM, Mike and Beebe settled into a famous old restaurant to sample the celebrated, roast suckling pig dinner. Everything was perfect, including the wine and dessert. Café solo and cognac followed to make it a memorable evening. But this night was far from being a happy and a celebrated one.

CHAPTER 13

Mike and Beebe left the restaurant feeling fat and sassy. With a great meal under their belts, they decided to walk the long block to the corner.

"We should be able to hail a taxi from there in no time," said Mike.

"This Flamenco place, is it far from here?" asked Beebe.

"I'll let the taxi driver find it for us. After all, that's his job."

Arm in arm they walked and finally reached the well lit intersection. People and cars made it a busy crossroads. Mike waited a few minutes, hoping to spot a taxi with its dome light shining, indicating it was available. Sure enough, a taxi approached and stopped where Mike and Beebe were standing. Mike reached for the rear door handle and opened it. At that time, from across the boulevard, a heavy four-door sedan sped at a two-hundred-eighty degree angle straight for their parked taxi. Mike, with his hand on the door knob, yelled, "Beebe . . . bac—" as the speeding sedan slammed into the parked taxi. The scream of tortured metal and broken glass filled the air. The violent impact hurled the taxi over the curb, with the right front and rear wheels resting on the sidewalk. Mike had pushed Beebe out of the way. She fell and tumbled into the gutter of the road, away from the wreck. The edge of the open taxi door slammed into Mike's left side and sent him painfully sprawling onto the sidewalk.

"Arrgh, son of a . . ." The pain shut off the remainder of his curse. He staggered to his feet and called out, "Beebe—where . . . are you okay?"

"Oh, look at my stockings. They're absolutely ruined!" Then, "Ouch, and my elbow hurts," was Beebe's groan. A few people helped her to stand up. The driver of the sedan forced his way out of his damaged car and although with an injured right leg, he stumbled, then ran. A witness pointed at a running figure that hobbled across the avenue, headed for a building doorway. Mike thanked the gentleman, and ignoring his pain, took after the perpetrator. Ignoring the traffic, and luckily not being stuck again by another motorist, he made it to the building that his assailant had entered. However, the huge, heavy, glass double doors were locked. Mike beat the glass with angry fists. Hearing the commotion, the building doorkeeper, *el portero* (a dying breed soon to be replaced by modern electronics), ran up and saw Mike's limp and the wretched condition of his torn jacket and pants leg. Not thinking whether or not Mike belonged in the building, the *portero* saw this as an emergency situation and quickly unlocked the door for the injured man.

"*Gracias.*" Showing pain, Mike thanked the *portero*, handed him some bills, and entered the apartment building. He hobbled through the wide marble foyer, then up two broad steps. In front of him were banks of three elevators along the ornate marbled wall. The area now split into two avenues, left and right.

Choosing left, Mike hobbled to another corner. He slowly inched forward and was just about to turn into it, when the assailant's arm swung downward with a serious club. Mike instantly stepped back, narrowly missing the blow. He quickly reached down and grabbed the wrist of his attacker and kicked his knee. "*Hijo de . . .*" was the painful reply. Mike twisted the captured arm and the man was now on one knee. Still holding onto his wrist, Mike stepped around and kicked the other leg of his assailant.

"Who are you? Who sent you?" Mike asked in Spanish. He kicked the man's leg again, and repeated, "*Who the hell sent you?*"

Before the downed man could reply, two pistol shots from the far hallway rang out. One struck the assailant in the head; the other narrowly missed Mike. He quickly released the captured arm and the attacker fell to the polished floor—quite dead. Mike ducked around the corner, knelt down low and peered down the long hallway. No one was in sight. After a few seconds, he decided to take the chance and stepped out into the well lit corridor, and ran for the entrance door. Luck would have it: an elderly woman was entering when Mike made it to the door. Beebe was outside as Mike charged out. He took her arm and said, "Let's get out of here, now."

"I heard some shots. Mike, what happened in there?" They rounded a corner, and kept walking fast as they heard the wailing of a police vehicle in the distance.

"Somebody shot the guy who ran into our taxi. But, are you all right?"

"I'm a little sore, but no real damage done here, except that my clothes are in a mess. What the heck is going on?"

"I don't know, honey," he answered and hailed an approaching taxi. "Let's get home—this night has turned into a gigantic nightmare."

CHAPTER 14

"Good Lord, Mike, you're badly bruised. Have you seen your left side?"

"Only about ninety percent." He groaned and tried to observe the entire injured area.

"Mother of mercy, you're black and blue, some yellow, and a bit of purple. And that's from your knee to your armpit. Get in bed now while I get some cold towels to help reduce that swelling." It was not a request, but a firm order from Beebe.

"You have a few bruises yourself, sweetheart."

"Perhaps, but not like yours, Mister Hero. I'll be jumping into bed with you in a moment. And believe me, tonight I really do have a headache."

"Damn it . . . me too."

The next morning Mike swallowed a couple of Panadol super capsules to help ease the pain that kept him in bed. Beebe was up and fixing breakfast after she called the company and reported that Mike would be out for a few days at least, due to an auto accident.

"*No, no, el está bien, pero con mucho dolor,*" was Beebe's final comuniqué with the director.

Mike tossed and turned due to unanswered questions that needed answers.

Who was that guy that ran into us last night? The attacker sped into our taxi at full speed and never hit the brakes. Why was he shot and killed? And what happened to Hilario? He certainly did not slip down those stairs. Why was blood found up near the top of the stairwell? Could he have been struck from behind and propelled down the steps? All these questions ran a marathon carousel around Mike's brain that kept him awake for some time. Despite the discoloration to his left side, the pain seemed to ease up considerably. By eleven, he was up, dressed, and made his way downstairs ready for a new day within the *Soul of Spain*.

CHAPTER 15

The old three-story house was situated just outside the main residential area of Irun. The city, located in the northern part of Spain, is a hop and a skip to the French southwestern border. This home was rented out by the American owner and his Spanish wife. They moved down to the small hillside town of Coin in the southern area of the country to enjoy the views of the Costa del Sol. Little did they realize what stories the walls of their former dwelling, now called a *safe house*, would reveal.

The safe house (*zulo)* was where many killings and other violent crimes were planned, which included bank robberies and kidnappings for ransom. In the *zulo*, six members of ETA gathered to plan their next attack. Some members of the Basque paramilitary group were trained by a number of North Ireland's IRA terrorist faction. The Basques' next target was again in Madrid.

Two women, Arantxa and Edurne, brought in a large plate of Idiazabal cheese and olives along with loaves of bread and set them on the table. Gorka Atxedonx, the oldest and leader of this group, gave a nod, and the men helped themselves to the *comida*. They also passed the wine bottles around to complete the meal, a mini celebration for the next attack.

CHAPTER 16

In the Top Secret lab in the basement of the General Products ESP building, three distinguished scientists and two renowned engineers were dressed in the decontamination suits. The three scientists stood at the center of the stainless steel table while the two engineers stood opposite them, all attention on the twelve-inch glass dome which housed the molten pink mass. Two additional tubes attached to the base of the dome for the injection of a mix of certain halogens and liquefied nitrogen would be applied at the proper time. The group could talk to each other and to the adjacent Control lab where all procedures would be executed by several computers controlling the timed events.

The lead Spanish scientist, Mateo Luis Delmundo, spoke into his attached microphone, "Gentlemen, and lady, we all reviewed these new procedures several times, along with the calculations and time events for this new test. Although we have had failures in the past, I maintain high hopes that we are on a track for eventual success. Let's hope this fresh approach will lead to new horizons." A murmured acceptance was uttered by the group.

"Before we start the sequence, Doctor Van Wollen, will you recite the procedures that will be taken?"

"Yes, of course. First—after the completed countdown, the Control computer will increase the voltage by seventeen percent, and the amperage by five. Total time for this operation will be twelve seconds. Immediately after, the liquid nitrogen mix with oxygen and hydrogen will be injected for five seconds, thus ending the new procedure. We should be able to see the results shortly after that."

"Exactly, very good," confirmed Delmundo, the lead scientist.

"Hello, Control. We are ready here. Give us a countdown when you are prepared to begin the new experiment."

"Yes sir, one moment please." After a short pause, Control announced, "A slow countdown now begins: five, four, three, two, one, initiate!"

After the first two seconds, there was a slight rumble at the base of the dome, then the start of a counter-clockwise movement of the molten pink mass. This was followed by a mist that obscured the movement within the glass dome. The addition of the higher voltage and current and then the injection of the liquid nitrogen caused a louder, more violent vibration and, finally, total silence when the computers completed the timed sequence of events. A slow, circular cloud that surrounded the mass finally dissipated, leaving a clear view of the dome's contents. A solid one-inch diameter candle-like structure, twelve inches high, was clearly visible within the glass dome. Smiles, then laughter followed by gloved hand shakes and a session of congratulatory messages echoed between the scientists, the engineers, and the Control room personnel.

"We've done it. Our new theories and calculations were correct," echoed the French female scientist, Madeleine Dubois.

Miss Dubois was a graduate honor student earning her PhD in biochemistry and biotechnology from the prestigious French engineering university, INSA Lyon. Although considered good-looking with a handsome figure, she had never married. Her ambition, her life, was dedicated to science. Jean-Pierre Bertrand Dubois, who taught a Materials Science and Engineering class at the university, could not convince his daughter, Madeleine, to consider marriage in hopes for grandchildren to carry on the family name. Madeleine closed that door in a heartbeat.

"Yes, we've achieved a monumental discovery that will improve explosive material forever," exulted an engineer.

It had been a four-year battle by some of the most brilliant people to develop, complete, and accomplish what had not existed yesterday.

"Hopefully, an improved explosive material will bring down any building that exists," added another scientist.

"The truth will be determined in tomorrow's first field test with this new material," said the happy lead scientist.

CHAPTER 17

Mike Keller, while carrying a cup of coffee, was returning to the ground floor elevators on route to his office. He was thinking of the slight rumble from yesterday that surprised some of the employees who suspected a minor earthquake. It only lasted a few seconds, with no aftershocks and no damage reported. He put it out of his mind.

At the same time, a group of about ten or eleven excited company personnel chatted and huddled together in an atmosphere reminiscent of energized party goers. They all passed in front of Mike, heading for the main exit doors. The group, all men and one woman wearing white lab coats, each carried a duffel bag. They exited the building, split up, and got into three company vehicles lined up for their use.

Hello, what's all this about? Who are these people and what's going on? Curiosity grabbed Mike's psyche and wouldn't let go. *What the hell, let's see what's causing such an excited rush.* He stopped briefly at the Security Desk and asked the guard who those people were that just left in such a hurry.

"*Lo siento*, I cannot give you their names, señor, but I can only say they are personnel from a laboratory in the basement," he apologized.

"*Muchas gracias*," said Mike as he hurried after the departing vehicles, tossing his coffee cup into a large trash bin just outside the main doors. *Now I'm glad I decided to be nosey. Basement lab, eh? This will be an interesting day, for sure,* thought Mike. He roared out of the parking lot in his new company car, and raced to catch a glimpse of the last SUV as it turned off the main avenue and headed for the dusty countryside roads. The large cloud of dust from the three vehicles ahead of him was the only evidence of their passage that Mike followed on this lonely, winding road heading northwest. He kept well behind, avoiding being detected. The drive lasted almost two hours when he slammed on his brakes, noting a sudden lack of dust clouds. The mid-morning air was clean and clear now, with that country grass smell that Mike always enjoyed when hunting or fishing.

He inched his car forward just around a turn and saw the three SUVs parked behind a high, three-sided concrete wall about fifty-five meters ahead of him. Putting his car in reverse, Mike drove back around the last turn, and parked. He got out and, partially hidden, observed the group putting on their decontamination gear. Mike thought, *Show time, but what?*

"Gentlemen, Miss Dubois, we had this field facility built some years back, before some of you came to our employ. This protective wall has a long, heavy, double shock-proof glass imbedded for forward viewing. Our experiments all failed, as you know, but with your expertise and specialized knowledge, we hope—with God's help—for a more successful day. As you all observed, we cut a three millimeter sliver of our product, now code-named *Candlelight,* and placed it into this small box. As you can see, two small antennas protruding just outside will accept the Execute signal when sent. The sample material is small as we don't really know what the outcome will produce—perhaps no more than that of a firecracker—upon which further larger slices will be taken and tested." The team gave a short laugh in unison.

"That old heavy truck was set out there some weeks ago, and luckily it's still intact." Delmundo, the lead scientist, held up the box containing the sliver of the new experiment in one hand for all to see. "Let us place our newborn *Candlelight* slice under the truck some seventy meters away from our protective shield. Again, we do not expect much of a bang from such a small sample. In any event, we'll be here to insure protection. *Si dios quiere,*" concluded Delmundo.

Although Mike was at least thirty or forty meters from the rear of the group, he could see them trudge out to the truck in the field. One of them placed the small box under the old vehicle, then all returned to the concrete and block shelter.

One of the Control staff produced a mobile UHF transmitter, capable of transmitting out-of-band signals over short distances, and handed it to Delmundo.

"The TX frequency was preset per your order last night, and the unit is charged and ready to operate. When ready, switch the unit to ON, verify the preset frequency, and press the transmit key to send the signal to our sample." He concluded with, "Good luck, sir."

"*Muchas gracias*, Victor." Delmundo held the transmitter, ensured everyone was behind the protective structure, and switched the unit to ON. After noting the frequency was correct, he gave a nod to each of his colleagues, turned to observe the distant truck through the protective reinforced glass, and pressed the TX switch.

What happened next was an unexpected, gargantuan, and terrifying explosion that hurled the truck twenty meters into the air. Secondary and tertiary explosions occurred in the air, completely shredding the truck while suspended. Unrecognizable small burning pieces of metal and rubber fell to the ground. All the personnel pressed their ears with their gloved hands for additional protection from the devastating explosions that followed. One of the engineers, in awe, stood up tall from the glass view port. Unfortunately, the shock wave that hit his head broke his neck and hurled his body approximately six meters backward. His death flight imitated a discarded, old rag doll, as he lay crumpled and dead among the partially grass-covered landscape. A huge cloud of colorless smoke rose above the unbelievable ten-meter-wide by five-meter-deep fissure and grave site. The falling burning debris was so small that not one piece of the truck, including the engine block, was recognizable; most of it simple disappeared. The extraordinary atomic-like detonation completely consumed the area and its contents around it. The resulting mini-mushroom cloud, as if sucked by a colossal vacuum, counter-clocked its way quickly down the cavernous hole, leaving the surrounding air clean and clear once again.

Mike, being further back from the main group, was partially hidden low behind a small hill, yet he was knocked off his feet. He immediately rolled into a ball, hands hard pressed over his ears, and hid behind his car for limited protection. In total disbelief at what he had just witnessed, Mike finally staggered upright and brushed himself off. Dazed and bleeding from his nose, he stumbled into his car, backed it up, pulled a U-turn and, in a confused and bewildered state of mind, headed back to civilization.

"My god, what — have — we — done?" asked the bewildered and shaken Madeleine Dubois. "What unholy evil have we just created?" She removed her decontamination head gear and looked at each of the remaining shocked group members.

"We were supposed to develop and improve the explosives used to bring down a commercial building, *not many city square blocks*," declared Doctor Van Wollen.

"Gentlemen, Miss Dubois, please be calm; this is not the time or place to discuss what just has happened here. Let us come together, retrieve the body of our colleague that fell and return to the lab. There we can analyze, dissect our findings and come to a rational and intelligent conclusion."

However, only Mateo Delmundo was privy to the true nature of the newly formed *Candlelight* experiment.

CHAPTER 18

"My dear Miss Dubois, when you telephoned earlier this evening that you needed to speak with me privately, I had no idea that you would be most upset." Delmundo's eyes never left Madeleine's every move as she nervously paced the living room of her elegant apartment. It was located six floors up in the infamous Doctor Fleming street area, just south of the Plaza Castilla.

"Indeed I am upset Señor Delmundo. I've spent my whole life in the best universities studying, learning and fulfilling my utmost desire to accomplish and achieve great strides to benefit nature and science." Delmundo, seated on a massive couch, tried to speak, but Madeleine held up a hand to interrupt his gesture and continued, "I cannot condone what we have produced. I will withdraw my papers, all calculations. . . The conversion between volumetric and mass flow-rate for gases, including the automatic estimation of gas density from molecular mass, well, was not at all by accident. My god, I helped define those parameters."

"Miss Dubois, we all contributed our knowledge and expertise in the development of our *Candlelight* product. Do you realize that we will all share in the wealth and fame of our achievement? Please understand that I cannot allow you to jeopardize our years of work and our history-making future. Right or wrong, we all must stick together in this venture."

"No. My conscience, my entire inner being, and my dedication to science will not allow me to continue with this unbridled project," said Madeleine.

Don Mateo Delmundo rose from the couch, his open hands pleading, "Miss Dubois, please take some time off and carefully reconsider your hasty decision. We definitely need you on our team to further continue our exploration of what this scientific achievement can do for us. Good or bad, we must carry on our research into this previously unknown domain."

Madeleine paced the floor back and forth while gesturing with her hands. She wore a fashionably styled pantsuit and a pair of low heel shoes. And although Delmundo eyed her as quite beautiful, he dismissed the vision with contempt and revulsion. He was becoming quite agitated and his jaw muscles began to twitch. *How can one so brilliant be so utterly stupid?*

"No, it is impossible for me to continue or contribute with this project any longer. I intend to expose it for what it is, this . . . this now insane, and highly dangerous development. Good Lord, what if we had used a five- instead of the three-millimeter sliver for the test? We all probably wouldn't be alive today!"

As she passed close by, Delmundo got up and quickly, seized her wrist and halted her parade.

"Stop, let go of me. You're hurting my arm!"

"Please be reasonable," he ignored her demand as she struggled to free her wrist. His strong grip jerked her closer to him as she futilely flayed at him with her free hand.

"Let me—" Madeleine's frantic plea was cut short by a vicious punch that split her lip and left her semi-conscious. She slumped to the floor while he still held her captured wrist.

"Damn you, Madeleine, damn you!"

In a final weak and desperate move, she attempted to kick his leg. It was a feeble and ineffective effort to fight back.

"Why didn't you listen to me? See how you made matters worse?" Standing dominantly over the fallen scientist, Delmundo bent down and repeatedly punched Madeleine's head until she no longer offered resistance to his attack. "Look at what you made me do! Now you'll have time to think this over." He straightened up, brushed his silver-white hair back into place, and wrapped his bloody and bruised fist with a handkerchief.

For a brief instant, Madeleine moved her arm and one leg in a challenge to crawl, but suddenly she lay quiet and motionless on the carpeted floor. Her once attractive face, already showing brutal signs of the punishing blows, was now an ugly mask. Delmundo, seeing her previous attempt to move, quickly bent down and observed the now immobile woman more closely. He bolted upright as if shocked and surprised at this final curtain.

"My God, she is dead," his words were almost inaudible. He straightened up, put a fist to his mouth, and bit down on one finger, his breathing labored as he finally let out a long sigh. *She made me do it. This is not my fault. Oh, this is horrible! But, I must preserve the* Candlelight*! He would understand what I had done. He must, and why not?*

Regaining his composure, he quickly put on his coat, opened the front door, and noted the empty hallway. He quickly moved to a bank of elevators and pressed a down arrow. Before it arrived, he abruptly changed his mind and ran for the exit stairway sign. Although he saw no one in the hallway, he could not bet on an empty elevator. After sprinting down the six flights of stairs, Mateo Luis Delmundo pulled up his coat collar and left the apartment building completely unnoticed. He was pleased with his casual departure.

CHAPTER 19

Mike was recuperating from multiple bruises caused by the horrific explosion in the countryside a couple days ago. A doctor's cauterization of his nose had also finally halted the bleeding from small, ruptured capillary veins. He had remained away from the job for three days now. The taxi accident and now this time off from his work at General Products would take their toll on his upcoming performance review.

* * * * *

At the same time, the Basque terrorists were at their house, planning their next attack on a major police station just north of Madrid. Their group would travel south to set up a temporary safe house not far from their target. Their new objective was selected: the main police station in Colmenar. This was a favorite tactic to disrupt and kill the many policemen who waged the war against their separatist movement. The downtown police station at the Plaza del Sol in the center of Madrid had been attacked so often that it was decided to detour that area of heavily guarded paramilitary enforcement—for the time being.

Luck would have it that the terrorists found and rented a farm complex at the northern end of Colmenar, close to the city but far enough to be safe from prying eyes. Their two four-door sedans easily parked in a large adjoining barn. The farm, called *Las Higueras* for its figs, was one of the few remaining parcels to escape the urban sprawl of concrete and steel buildings that would soon populate the countryside. Gone would be the fate of all fig trees in the valley.

The six terrorists dressed in the clothes of a *granjero*, a farmer, to complete their disguise and to blend in with the local population—if ever the situation arose. Although they all spoke Spanish (and some English), their northern accents would stand out and draw attention to themselves.

It is not to say that they were stupid terrorists; on the contrary, most were educated and driven by an ingrained belief in their cause. In the meantime, it was prudent and necessary for them to remain at their rented farm until the time for the attack to take place.

CHAPTER 20

Andoni Bihox, at twenty-four years old the youngest member of this ETA group, hated this *zulo* and, because of his age, he felt a need to get out and participate in some excitement of a personal nature. Gorka had ruled that all would remain at the farmhouse until the time to strike became available. The other older members, well trained, did not need to be told twice.

"Gorka, I am suffocating in this *finca*. I need to get out for at least a short time," pleaded Andoni.

"No," Gorka's answer was short and final.

"Look, I will drive a short distance and very slowly to make sure not to cause attention. Please Gorka; I promise not to make any trouble. Just give me a chance to get out of this . . . this prison for just a little while. Have I caused you any problems in the past?" Gorka put down his wine glass, stood up, and looked at Andoni—eye to eye.

"If it weren't for your father—I promised him to look after you. He told me you needed a bridle to rein you in once in a while. However, you have proven yourself to be reliable when I needed you in the past. If I let you go for just two hours, will that satisfy you and guarantee me that nothing will follow you here and jeopardize our entire mission?"

"That I promise you, Gorka, I will be like a mouse, nice and quiet, and you will have my utmost gratitude." Andoni gave his leader a firm hug, as Gorka reluctantly handed him the car keys.

"Andoni, bring back some groceries, and be very careful," advised the leader. With a smile and a wave of his hand, Andoni acknowledged the order, and headed for the large garage/barn beside the main house. Although he exited the barn in a slow, controlled manner, his heart and imagination began to ignite, heat up, and run wild.

CHAPTER 21

"Hello, hello!" Brandson screamed into the telephone. "What the hell is going on over there, Michael? Another employee found dead, possibly murdered? This time a woman scientist! Do I have to come over there and take charge of every damn situation? Frankly Michael, I'm getting all ugly reports that will devastate our position out there despite our overall progress and profit reports."

"It's true, Charles, that there are a lot unexplained events going on here, and I must say, it'll take me and the local police some time to figure it all out." Michael wasn't making excuses, but just telling the truth.

"I don't want ifs, and, or buts. I want resolution and conclusion! Do I make myself perfectly clear Michael?"

Before he could give Charles an answer, Charles Brandson slammed the phone down and terminated the overseas call.

Damn it all, what next? Brandson's fierce temper caused the blood vessels to engorge in his neck and temples. He pushed some important pagers into his attaché case and called his secretary.

CHAPTER 22

Andoni eased the big sedan out from the dirt road and easily turned onto the paved street that headed to the fringes of the northern city's neighborhoods. He took deep breaths repeatedly and silently thanked Gorka for this needed time off. Oh, he would not stop to take alcohol and possibly jeopardize the group with disclosure. Although a hothead, he considered himself a loyal, upstanding member and would fight to the death in preparation for final victory. Yes, he was a loyal ETA member, young but vulnerable. Andoni drove with the window glass down, letting the breeze run through his jet black hair and taking in large amounts of country-sweetened air. His handsome features relaxed as he longed for some excitement in his life. Little did he realize that his wish would soon be granted.

* * * * *

Beebe was stretching her legs out in a comfortable jog and thought about cutting her daily run along this sparsely populated area and heading for home. She wore shorts (slowly being accepted by Spanish morals) along with running shoes and a halter top that tied at her neck and slim waistline.

Andoni took an unplanned turn and drove easily down the road when he spotted Beebe jogging along at a comfortable pace. *Ai madre, que piernas! Oh mother, what legs!* Andoni's internal heat rose as he slowed and took in the flashing long legs of Beebe. Many Spanish men consider it a duty to conquer a fair-skinned female tourist. His breathing also quickened as he bit into his lip, then flexed his jaw muscles; not to say his loins were also becoming activated. He pulled his car up alongside Beebe's stride, rolled down the passenger window, and called out, "Do you speak English? I can give you a lift to wherever you are going."

"No thank you," Beebe replied without turning her head, but took in a peripheral view of the car. This scenario happened several times even in the States. She kept up her run while Andoni stopped the car. He took quick notice of the sparse neighborhood, and saw Beebe continuing her jog. Andoni was now thinking with his inflamed desire, and not with his head. He drove up fast just ahead of Beebe, turned the car into her intended path, stopped, and quickly slid out the passenger side of his vehicle. Beebe came to a halt and now began to worry about this intruder.

"*Señorita, por favor*, I only wish to know you better." Andoni smiled and held up his open hands to signal his dubious intent and also, to stop her forward progress.

"And you, Señor, I do NOT care to know YOU better," Beebe held up her ring finger to indicate her marital status, and hoped that would defuse the tense situation.

She tried to rush passed him but he grabbed her wrist and swung her toward him. Beebe lashed out with her free hand but he also caught it, and tightened his grips. She tried to kick him but he quickly turned her right arm making her miss her target as Andoni dragged and pushed her into the passenger side of the car.

"No, no!" she screamed and struggled to free herself. His physical strength and determination prevented her escape. Before she could think of a defensive strike, Andoni beat her to it. With a quick move he let her go of one hand, and drove a hard fist into her face that rendered Beebe stunned, venerable, and in pain.

"*Sí, sí, señora*, but you are now in my country, and I make the rules." Andoni shoved her onto the floor of the car and in so doing took liberties in pawing at her smooth skin. He then jumped into the driver side, and spun a quick U-turn while making sure Beebe could not be seen by outside viewers. Part of Beebe's lower leg was up on the seat, and Andoni again reached and caressed her with a rough hand. She instantly withdrew into a fetal position on the floor. Andoni was now fully determined to have his way with this foreign lady, as he drove the route back to the farm.

He didn't slow down crossing the railroad tracks, and then made a wild left turn onto the dirt road leading down the valley to their rented *zulo*. After a minute, and after making another left turn and avoiding several pot holes in the dirt road, Andoni turned right and pulled up in front of the barn. Exiting the car, he set the automatic locks on all doors to keep Beebe inside the vehicle. He then ran and opened the two huge doors of the barn, returned to the car and drove it into the old wooden building.

After getting out, he unlocked the passenger side door, roughly yanked Beebe out, and physically threw her onto a pile of hay within an empty stall. Andoni's handsome face was awash with anticipation, his eyes flashing with lust, especially so after seeing his prize in such a defenseless position.

"Don't you come near me." Beebe, now aware of the inexcusable circumstances, found some commanding firmness as she scooted back as far as possible along the hay-covered floor. She was now in for the fight of her life.

Inside the main house, Gorka asked, "I heard the car come back. Did Andoni bring in any *comida?*" The rest of the men were at the table playing cards, and, with a few disgruntled negatives, *No, nada* was their answer.

"Damn that young one, I told him to go to the *tienda* for some shopping." Gorka stormed out of the main house and headed for the barn.

* * * * *

Many miles away, an elderly gentleman also made his way for an appointment. He was chauffeured to the local international airport, where his departure was uncomplicated and made flying once again a pleasure to experience, even with the TSB new rules. He was, however, a troubled man as he was escorted to his private seat in his company's twin-engine jet aircraft. A single flight attendant would see that the passenger's wishes and comfort were attainable. After a six-and-a-half-hour smooth flight, the jet was cleared to land at Madrid's International airport. After taxing up to an awaiting limousine, Charles H. Brandson exited the plane and swiftly entered the waiting vehicle. The sign on the driver's door panel proclaimed, **General Products, España S.A.**(Sociedad Anónima).

CHAPTER 23

Gorka swung open the barn doors, after hearing a muffled struggle along with a female's determined cry for help, picked up an old broom stick handle, and ran to investigate the occurrence. Within a stall, Andoni was on top of Beebe and struggling to separate her clothes from her body. She prayed while fending off the attacker that it would not happen.

With all the force that he could muster, Gorka struck a blow to Andoni's back while grabbing a handful of his hair and pulled the attacking youth off Beebe.

"Andoni, you stupid fool, what have you done? You just may have put at risk our—" Gorka quickly cut short his outrage. Andoni, now on his back and holding up his hands, tried to escape the additional blows delivered by his leader.

"No, Gorka, no. Please, *no más*. You are killing me."

"Get into the house, *an-i-mal*." Gorka stretched the animal insult to young Andoni.

Beebe struggled and stood up while rearranging her tattered clothes and brushing away bits of hay.

"Get out, you ungrateful *bastardo*," was Gorka's last comment to the injured Andoni, who limped and cursed his way out of the barn.

"Are you hurt, madam?" he asked after noticing her ring finger. Beebe shook her head while leaning on the back wooden wall, her arms crossed across her chest. "I am so very sorry that this has happened. These young men of today don't know the meaning of decency and control. But I assure you, he will be further punished by the others in the house. Please try to forget this incident, and believe me his punishment will be most severe. Allow me to drive you to your home or wherever you wish." Gorka's apology was sincere as he then dropped the broom handle to the stall floor and motioned Beebe to another vehicle with an extended open hand. She was reluctant to enter another car again for fear of her intolerable recent experience. "Please, you have no cause for alarm, as I give you my word of honor. You will be safe."

As Gorka drove out, he insisted Beebe scoot down in her seat to avoid any onlookers. He motioned her to regain her upright position after they were on the main paved road, and arrived to where she was first assaulted.

"Please, do not report this to the police as it will bring such disgrace to the family. Again, I say that young man will be severely punished for the shame and dishonor he brought to our family." Beebe nodded her agreement and asked him to stop several block from her home. Somehow, she did not want to let him, or anyone, know where she lived. Gorka let her out and, with his hand over his heart, he proclaimed, "*Por favor*, please forget this all happened. Again, I say the young one will receive additional punishment for his unacceptable behavior." Beebe gave a nod as Gorka U-turned and drove away. She quickened her walk and looked back several times to make sure she was not followed.

After getting into her home, Beebe headed straight for the shower. She stripped off all her clothes, cranked up the hot water and stepped in. Although she scrubbed herself with soap and a rough cloth, she had a chill shiver and tried to forget her recent duel with an almost disastrous event. After the lengthy shower, then toweling herself dry, she thought, *Should I tell Mike? Maybe not. He would surely go ballistic. Forget about it. All this never happened.*

A block away, the occupant of a car saw Beebe enter the locked gate that fronted her house. Gorka was satisfied that his vigilant search had paid off.

CHAPTER 24

"Hey Beebe, I'm home." Michael dropped off his attaché case, shook off his suit jacket, and loosened his tie. "Sweetheart, you'll never guess who dropped into Madrid today. Okay, forget all the guess work. It was the old man himself, Charles H. Brandson, and he gave me a reaming out, to be sure."

"Be right there," answered Beebe. She entered the living room wearing a silky bathrobe and smelling like sweet jasmine in the springtime. She approached him slowly, her head down, then quickly rushed to Mike, sobbing with tears staining her swollen cheek. Beebe hugged him so hard that he knew something was terribly wrong.

"Just hold me Mike. Hold me and don't ever let go."

"Hey, hey there, what's going on?" He held her at arm's length. "Holy mother of . . . What happened to you? Come here and sit down, and tell me who, what, where, and when."

Beebe found the control she needed through Mike's strong and comforting embrace. She stopped sobbing, dried her tears with a tissue, and started a random accounting of her day's experience.

"Hold on, honey, back up and take your time. Start at the beginning where all this initiated. Take it easy and try to remember every damn little detail—it's so very important. And most of all, describe the person who did this to you."

With patience Beebe recounted all the painful occurrences from the time she was about to finish her daily jog. Her tears started to well up again when she retold what happened in the barn. She was using another tissue as she concluded with an older man driving her back to where she was forced into a car.

Mike stroked her hair, gently kissed her swollen cheek, and slightly blackened eye. They held an embrace for a long time. Mike's rage roared within his mind and heart.

*I'll hunt you down whoever you are, you bastard. I **will kill you** for sure.*

He led Beebe into the kitchen and prepared an ice pack to ease her pain, and some hot tea to calm her down. Aspirin tablets were also on the menu. They sat together at the kitchen table—Beebe with an ice pack held to the side of her face, and Mike with murder on his mind.

"Tomorrow morning Beebe, I promise you, **we will** go hunting."

CHAPTER 25

The next morning, the sun broke out early and promised a warm and clear summer day. Beebe was dressed in slacks and a light blouse, with a silk scarf around her slender neck. Although she was almost ready to forget the entire episode because her cheek swelling was reduced and, with Mike's nursing, her pain had subsided, she decided to play this day out. Mike wore his hunting boots, short-sleeve shirt, and a Redskins football cap. He carried a notebook to his car and led Beebe to the passenger seat.

"Okay, sweetheart, from the beginning, show me where you were picked up and forced into *Macho Man*'s car. I want to be in the exact direction and location where this all started. Are you okay?" Beebe gave a nod and indicated the direction to the site, which was a few blocks away. After getting his car parked in the spot where Beebe had been kidnapped, Mike turned in his seat and faced her.

"Look, honey, what I'm going to say and do will depend on your input. This may sound crazy to you now, but please try to be in the exact position on the floor of this car—close your eyes if it will help—and try to describe whatever you felt, time-wise, or thought of, from the moment he began to drive with you in his car. I was going to bring a pillow for you, but thought it best to enact the closest experience you had yesterday; sorry, sweetheart."

Beebe understood what her husband was trying to do, and placed herself on the floor of their car. Mike looked down at his wife and thanked God he had the woman of his dreams: beautiful, brave, and true. "Okay, Bee, think, and let me know when you're ready."

She gave a weak smile and said, "All right, Mike, let's try to find that SOB. He first made a sharp left U-turn from here and drove a few minutes in that direction."

"Did he drive fast?"

"I don't think so—maybe 30, 40 miles an hour. And that's a guess. Somewhere along here I felt a long right hand curve, and then crossing some bumps like railroad tracks." Mike indeed saw the curve and then the rail tracks. As he drove over them, Beebe said, "Yes, yes, that made my head bump up against the firewall. Keep going, Mike."

"Good girl, you're doing just fine." Beebe closed her eyes and desperately tried to imagine what the road would look like.

"We're coming up to an old intersection, left or right?"

"Right, I think. No, Mike, make a left turn! I could feel the dirt road here, and smell the dust." Mike slowed down and maneuvered over the country dirt road trying to avoid the pot holes. "There was another sharp left turn somewhere in this time frame, and I could tell we definitely were in the farming countryside. Mike, I'm not sure, but I think we made another left turn, bumpy road, then a right turn and stopped. The next thing I knew, I was flat on my back in a barn stall."

Mike slowed down and observed the picturesque land and its surroundings. There were several far out farm buildings in the distance, but only one that appeared close to where Beebe's guess-work fit. He slowly drove past a large farm house with an adjacent barn off to one side. A right turn there would put Beebe's account in place. *Could this be the rat's nest?*

Mike drove some fifty yards down the dirt road without seeing any other farm houses or barns.

"What do you think?" he asked Beebe.

"I don't remember that the turn-off from the country road was this long. Could you drive back to the farm house you first saw?"

"Okay, I'll start from there and you try to tell how much time it took when you returned to that main road. Do you think you can do that?"

"I'll give it a try," as she scooted down low on the front seat floorboard, her head resting on the car door. When Mike just returned to the farm house, he said,

"Time it from HERE to the main paved road." After he drove up the dirt grade road to the turn-off, Mike stopped the car and faced

Beebe. "What do you think, Bee, can you remember if that was the way you felt it?"

"I'm pretty sure that was it, Mike. In fact, I'm damn positive." Mike turned his head around, looked down the dirt road, and confirmed that the distant farm house did indeed have a large barn off to the side and nestled about ten meters beside and just below the main house. There was, however, no visible activity in the area.

"Ya done good, sweetheart." It was a favorite expression of his to compliment his wife. "Let's get back to the house after I take a couple of notes on all this terrain. Can you think of anything else?"

After straightening up on the passenger seat, Beebe confirmed, "Yes, the man who drove me back said something about 'the others' in the house. Could there be a gang of them?"

Putting away his notebook, Mike embraced his wife and gave her a kiss, and added, "Let's go—I've got some serious planning to do."

CHAPTER 26

The next morning, Mike was making his way to Brandson's office when he thought he recognized someone just leaving that same room. *What is it?—That silver-gray hair? Where have I seen that figure?* Just before he opened the door, Mike turned and looked back at Mateo Luis Delmundo who hurried around a corner of the marble hallway. As he entered Brandson's office, Mike realized that he needed to clear his mind while meeting with Brandson. He managed to do just that, obtaining praise from the CEO for his contributions, despite the sick-leave time off.

Mike spent the rest of the day cleaning up some details of his project, which was under budget and on time. Toward the end of the work day, Mike stood in front of the large picture window in his office looking out at the passing traffic and also observing the local parking lots. It was during this brief interlude with his arms folded, and leaning against the edge of his window frame that his long term memory kicked in with a faint picture of the silver-haired man. The parked cars in the parking lot supplied the memory trigger—three parked vehicles in a desolate country environment. It came into focus. *Yes, that's the lead man at the explosion site. I'm sure that was him. But what was he doing coming out of Brandson's office? What does each have to discuss? Was it that horrendous explosion, or some other Top Secret project? What the hell is going on?*

CHAPTER 27

The next day, with a good description of Beebe's assailant etched in his brain, Keller parked his car on the high ridge that afforded a perfect view of the suspected farmhouse less than two kilometers below. He didn't care to miss several days work in order to find the *Macho Man* who had attacked Beebe. Getting to his prey was the paramount deed burning in his soul. Mike would use whatever means, weapons, and hunting abilities to get to his prey. *God forgive me.*

He used a pair of high-powered binoculars to periodically scan the farm house for any movement. He also noted that there were no animals or crops growing or any that would need attention in the surrounding fields. *Yes, this has to be the place,* he assured himself. *But, what the hell are they doing here, if not farming?*

* * * * *

After a few hours of vigilant focus on the farmhouse, and noting the sign above the main door, *"Las Higueras,"* Mike decided to take a break. He set his binoculars on the seat beside him, tucked his cap over his eyes, and slouched down behind the wheel for a needed reprieve.

Bad luck would have it: at that exact time, a black sedan loaded with four ETA terrorists exited out of the barn and drove up to the main road. As they approached Mike's car, the driver slowed down and stopped alongside the napping man's car. The four terrorists looked at Mike as he sprang up, completely awake, and tilted his cap. He gave the four sets of eyes burning into his skull a quick, short salute, tucked his cap back down over his face, and took a wild chance he would be dismissed as a non-threatening casual tourist.

Mike breathed easier, but his heart was racing as the black sedan finally geared up and proceeded on its course toward the city. Mike had just a few short seconds to observe that group, and it was fresh in his memory. Was it like an old movie you saw years ago but were now trying to remember where you had seen a recognized face? Or was it a stand-out in a crowd that shocked your memory?

He put the image out of his mind, and watched the black sedan pull away and head for the main road. Mike decided to keep up a vigil on the farmhouse. He scanned the dwelling and the surrounding area again, and again. Before he could put down the binoculars, that damn black car pulled up in a heap of road dust beside Mike's car. The four occupants leaped out, two on each side, and jerked both front doors open and pulled Mike out.

"*Hijo de puta!*" said a Basque.

Mike also said it to himself. *Son of a bitch! Big bad hunter man, you really screwed up this time. I should have seen them coming. Damn!*

On gaining his footing, Mike struck out and hit one attacker in his solar plexus, causing him to crumple to the dusty road. A vicious punch came from behind and stunned Mike enough for another terrorist to smash Mike square on the chin. He went down for the full count—the binoculars still hung around his neck when he hit bottom.

CHAPTER 28

Mike woke up with a headache which got him into a bad mood, which got worse when he realized he was tied hands and feet to a wooden post in a barn. Bales of unused hay lined several stalls, and an assortment of farm tools hung from the old wooden walls. A pail of water was splashed across Mike's head, bringing back the encounter with the four strangers from the dirt road. He shook his head and focused on the man in front of him.

"Well now, Señor Michael Lamont Keller, please tell me why you were caught spying on my farm this morning." Gorka kept flipping Mike's wallet to the open then closed position as he circled around his captive opponent.

"Name, rank, and serial number, is all you'll get from me, you bastard." Mike's reply was accompanied with an unsuccessful struggle to free his bonds.

"I see from your temporary driver's license that your address in 585 Mirasierra Road—not very far from here." As soon as the words came out of Gorka's mouth, he stopped his movement just in back of Mike's tied-up position.

Of course! La Rubia, the American woman that Andoni brought here. Hijo de puta. I know their house! Gorka gathered his thoughts, faced Mike, and returned the wallet to Mike's pocket.

"Let me make a guess, Mister Keller: you have a beautiful young wife who was recently, ah, let's say . . . entertained by one of my men. Am I correct?" Again, Mike strained at his bonds until his wrists and ankles became painful. "And now," Gorka continued, waving a hand in the air, "you bravely but foolishly decided to play the justified husband seeking revenge for a young man's mistake. Oh, I do admit that his act was wrong, and my man was disciplined for his lustful stupidity, but, really now, no deadly harm came to your wife, a little bruise here and there, but nothing serious, I am sure."

Mike clenched his teeth and spoke, "Why not let me be the judge, jury, and executioner?"

"With a shotgun from the back seat of your auto?"

"I always go prepared for the worst."

"Oh no, Señor Keller, you will not be the executioner here. For it seems YOU are at your worst end. And I am now troubled with the question of what to do with you."

Mike stared at Gorka and said, "Just let me get my hands on your Mister *Macho Man* and later, you and I can discuss our options."

"I do suppose you do have the right to avenge the attack on your wife, and that puts me in an awkward position." Gorka tapped his nose for a few seconds, made a decision, and then faced Mike with a proposal. "If I introduce you to the man you wish to confront, do I have your word when you finish punishing him that you will be satisfied and forget this entire, unfortunate matter?"

"I agree, you have my solemn word," said Mike.

"Be advised, my man is a young, strong worker. You will, as they say in English, 'have your hands full.' However, if you should accidently or otherwise kill him, that would involve a troubling police situation. Therefore, *you will die* before this day is over. I promise you that, Señor Keller. Do I make myself clear?"

"Yes, perfectly clear."

"I have now important business to attend to. My associates will attend to your morbid desire. Good-bye, Mister Keller, and good luck with your morbid desire." Gorka turned and left the barn, trailing a short, sinister laugh.

A short time later, Mike was still tied to the post when three other terrorists enter the wooden building. One who was younger, good looking, and more physically fit than the other two, stepped back and allowed another to come forward and cut the ropes to free Mike. All three men showed knives in sheaths attached to their belts. Mike stepped forward and massaged his wrists as he maneuvered around the threesome. From Beebe's description, Mike pointed at the handsome one and whispered, "*Macho Man*," and, with his right hand, he motioned for him to step forward. Instead, one of the other men came ahead, shaking his finger to indicate a NO response. He advanced towards Mike and bravely gave a rapid fake, one-two punch. He was rewarded by a flashing kick to his outside leg and a solid punch to his jaw. Dazed, he fell to the dusty barn floor and remained there. Terrorist number two came at Mike with a burst of speed and swinging fists left and right. Mike parried these blows with his arms and snuck in a few of his own punches. The terrorist stepped back and charged again. Mike moved to one side and used his attacker's forward motion to his advantage. Mike ducked under a wild punch, grabbed the attacker's full head of hair, and slammed it against one of the stall's supporting wooden posts. Although dazed and disoriented, he didn't go down. Mike punched at his kidneys, spun him around, and executed a crippling blow to this terrorist's face. Terrorist number two went comatose and sank to the dirty wooden floor.

All this time, *Macho Man* studied the American's moves, and nodded his appreciation, for he too was schooled in the martial arts of self defense. As Mike circled around to confront *Macho Man*, terrorist number one rose up on one knee and sneered. He was rewarded with a side kick to his head. He went down again and didn't move. *Macho Man* then ripped off his shirt and revealed a well-built, muscular upper body. Mike also removed his shirt to compliment and match his opponent's physique. Each combatant eyed the other looking for a flaw, a physical defect that would benefit him in combat. Although Andoni Bihox, aka *Macho Man*, was one inch taller and a few pounds heavier than Mike, they each secretly admitted that they were both able and fit for battle.

As they slowly circled each other, Mike doubled his fists and poured every ounce of force and fury into his hands of vengeance. He thought of Beebe and the horror she had endured. *Come, Macho Man, and meet your punisher. It's time for retribution.*

As Andoni advanced, Mike took his fighting stance, his feet apart for balance and his fists ready for combat. However, the first blow came from Andoni. It was a surprisingly fast, straight jab that caught Mike's cheek. A smile from Andoni provided him with a good start. The two combatants circled each other with deadly intentions. This time it was Mike's chance to land a solid punch that caused a tooth to fly out of Andoni's mouth. That action was followed by both men exchanging punches and vicious kicks. A small cut appeared on Mike's forehead, and dark swelling started to emerge on Andoni's face. Both men were tangled in a bloody fight that would certainly produce only one victor.

Back and forth they traded blows when a flying roundhouse kick from Mike sent the *Macho Man* sprawling on the musty barn floor. Andoni spied a long-handled pitchfork a few feet away and scrambled to use it as a weapon. Both men now crouched; Andoni feinted with a stabbing attack, quickly switched ends and struck a power blow to Mike's ribs, causing him to fall. Andoni advanced, stood over Mike and, holding the pitchfork high, drove it down to impale his victim. But Mike quickly turned, and the steel tines buried themselves into the wooden floor. He then reached up, held onto the metal tine support, and with a swift leg up-kick, Mike shattered the long handled tool into two pieces. With half of the pitchfork still buried into the floor, Mike rolled away and again regained an upright position. Andoni advanced, swinging his new found club, and Mike ducked, landing a few solid punches at his attacker. Before Andoni could reset his next swing, Mike executed a spinning back-fist punch that caught his opponent high on his forehead, thus causing a massive cut that sent blood flying in a half circular pattern.

Although now bleeding from head, nose, and mouth, Andoni regained his senses and, with a growl and hatred in his eyes, he jumped up and with surprising speed charged at Mike. The severe impact took both warriors up against and through the old barn's back wall, sending splintered wood shards out onto the late afternoon ground. Mike caught the impact from the wall with Andoni falling on top of him. Mike tried to get up but was too dazed at that moment. Andoni rolled off and quickly withdrew the knife from his belt. With Mike's back in full view Andoni screamed and attacked—his knife high in the air.

Have you ever heard a metal shovel hit a big solid rock? That was the sound the shovel made—*thwang*—when it hit Andoni square on the back of his head, which ended the fight. Mike turned around and shook his head to make sure his vision was cleared and not impaired. Beebe stood there holding a long-handled shovel, making sure Andoni didn't move. He lay face down in the dirt, motionless.

"Beebe, what the . . . how did you . . .?" Mike staggered to his wife and they embraced.

"Oh, Mike, you're bleeding. You're hurt."

"It's not so bad. How did you get here?"

"When you didn't come home, I put on my jogging gear and took a chance and ran to the hill overlooking this farm. When I didn't see your car up there, I continued down here and prayed no one would see me coming. I knew you might be in trouble because the keys were still in your car parked back here. You would never let that happen. I heard the fight going on and grabbed this shovel for protection. I didn't know what to expect. Then you two came crashing out."

"Good girl, Bee—let's get out of here."

"But, Mike, you're bleeding".

"Later, sweetheart. Come on."

"That's the guy who attacked me, the SOB."

"There's no time to dwell on his condition. Let's go before the others come out to investigate."

They rushed to his car, got in, and drove away, sending up a cloud of dirt and dust until they hit the main road.

Mike made a turn that puzzled Beebe. Before she could speak, Mike said, "We're going to try to spend the night at Ramón's house, just in case—those characters back there know where we live and might decide to do their own house hunting."

* * * * *

Ramón and his wife, Pilar, gladly took Mike and Beebe in for the night. After they cleaned up, Mike filled Ramón in on what had transpired just a short time ago. Ramón was shocked and horrified by Mike's encounter with the farm's inhabitants.

Before retiring for the night, Ramón handed Mike two handguns from his personal collection.

Late next morning, Mike and Beebe returned to their home. He changed into his suit and sported a band-aid high over his eye. Beebe also was dressed and ready to accompany him. Although it was already mid-morning, Mike hoped it would be just a normal day at work. It would be far from it.

CHAPTER 29

Before Mike could settle into his office, a secretary informed him of an urgent meeting with Charles Brandson.

When Mike entered Brandson's office, he was surprised to see Ramón Fuentes standing beside Brandson's desk.

"Come in, come in," Charles waved a hand at Mike who approached, smiled at Ramón, and shook his hand. "Gentlemen, you may sit down if you wish," gestured the CEO, directing them to leather-covered comfortable chairs. "First of all, a few hours ago, Ramón told me the harrowing story of what you and your wife have been through. The actions of your attackers were unforgivable, and unacceptable. By the way, how is Beebe?"

"Beebe's just fine. A bit shaken up, but she's a fighter. I've got her parked in my office right now."

"Hold on a second." Charles spoke into the intercom. "Paula, get Mrs. Keller from Mike's office and bring her up here."

"*Sí, señor, ahora mismo.*"

When Beebe arrived at Brandson's office, he quickly noted the healing bruises on her face as she took a chair next to Mike. It pained Charles to the point that a few tears appeared around his eye lids. He was visibly shaken, and with sustained strength he turned to the report in front of him. After a brief pause to regain composure, he began.

"You should be pleased to note that our local police along with the *Guardia Civil* have concluded a raid on that farmhouse and have taken all six men and two women into custody. All were found to be terrorists of the ETA group from the north—mainly from Irun city. One of the men was taken to the hospital, where he remains in a critical and unstable mental condition." On hearing this report, Mike and Beebe looked at each other. Mike gave her a quick wink and thought, *From Macho Man to Vegetable Man—have a nice day!*

"It appears that you two were instrumental in breaking up that terrorist group, and you are hereby commended as heroes by the mayor of the city. Congratulations." Charles ended his speech and extended a hand to Mike and Beebe, which they each took and simply said, "Thank you."

Charles got up, faced the group, and said, "Ramón, will you and Mrs. Keller please leave now, as I must speak privately with Michael." Ramón nodded and led Beebe to the door.

Now alone with Michael, Charles went to his efficiently hidden liquor cabinet, offering, "How about a drink, Michael? You certainly deserve one."

"Okay, just a short one—a scotch and soda, if available," replied Mike as he approached the cabinet.

"No problem, my main man. I have all the comforts of home at my disposal." Charles fixed the drink, turned, and handed a full glass to Mike. "As you know, with rank comes privilege. I salute you, Michael Keller, for being on my team." They raised their glasses. "You've just earned yourself a promotion and a twenty percent pay raise. But, with an increase in corporate promotion and additional responsibilities, comes a solid commitment to accept and undertake an unfailing and unquestionable loyalty to its leader. Do you understand what I'm saying, Michael?"

Perplexed, Mike set his drink down and answered, "Yes, I understand what you're saying, and I certainly appreciate the promotion and the huge unexpected pay raise, but I can't help wondering what you're getting at—that is, what more do you expect of me? You already have my commitment and loyalty. . ."

Charles waved a hand and said, "Sit down, Michael; I need to tell you a story, a real horror story." Charles returned to his chair behind his desk, sat down, and began. "Almost twenty years ago, an ETA terrorist bomb was detonated that killed five Spanish law officers and several innocent by-standers here in Madrid. I still have the newspaper article and the pain in my heart of that cowardly, vicious, and murderous act." Mike shifted in his chair and gave Charles his full attention. "You see,

Michael, the by-standers killed ... were my wife and two teenage daughters on a shopping trip in that area. The bomb blast torn them to pieces, and so set off a very dark bloody spot in my heart and soul. I've lived with this burning hatred for ETA, and for my revenge, ever since."

"Oh, my God," Mike sat up and continued, "I am so very sorry, Charles. I don't know what to say . . ."

Charles raised one hand and downed the rest of his drink with his other.

"You see, Michael, for the past twenty years or so, I've dedicated my life to a journey of revenge and the complete extermination of the ETA organization. I'm glad you are on my team. However, I am going to ask you to join my special group to help me wipe out this terrorist main business headquarters in the north. There have been many obstacles in my planned journey to this point, but I will prevail. Oh yes, I promise you that."

Mike sat down and put his drink aside. He gathered his thoughts and presumed assumptions which began to appear from the recent past.

"And the murder of Hilario Fuentes—was that in your plans, Charles?"

"Oh, for God's sake, Michael, that unfortunate incident was a mistake, a flaw, which I regret."

"The mistake was that I was the intended victim, am I correct so far?"

Charles came around the corner of his massive desk, sat on a corner and looked down at Michael.

"Listen to me carefully, Michael, for this is the truth. I did not know much about you then, and you were caught in an unauthorized area and in doing so became an enemy to my project. But that is all in the past. It's history now that you've seen my Candlelight experiment in action. The three-millimeter slice of my Candlelight recent test in the countryside was only a minute sample of what I can do."

Before Charles Brandson could continue with his insane plan of destruction, Mike sat up and said, "My wife and I were run down in a taxi, and someone shot at me that same night. Was that also part of your plan to silence me?"

"But, Michael, don't you understand? You were indeed my enemy—at that time." Charles got up and walked unhurriedly about the room, waving his hand as if to clear the air of all past discussions. "You are NOT my enemy now. I consider you as a true team member. Hell, you just single-handedly wiped out an ETA cell right here in Madrid. I'm proud of you, Michael, as you now know personally what that evil group can, and will, do. I certainly hope you are capable of understanding my position, and why I had to protect, defend, and carry on with my solution to their madness."

"And the murder of Madeleine Dubois—also an excuse to defend your unthinkable bomb?" questioned Mike.

"My successful Candlelight experiment will give a brilliant light to Spain, and the world will be a more peaceful and safer place to live, and no one, not even Miss Dubois, would deter me from that objective. Mateo Delmundo made a hasty decision to safeguard our newly completed Candlelight device. Unfortunate for Madeleine, but it had to be done. Furthermore, as the Spanish government cannot do the job, then someone has to take control and get it done. I'm asking for your help, Michael. This is my destiny."

Before Mike could consider a reply, Charles continued in a soft and mellow voice, "I won't need your answer right now; sleep on it, Michael, talk it over with your wife, and let me know your answer in the morning, and think of what all this means to me personally."

"Charles, just how do you propose to select just the ETA group for your extermination?"

"They are everywhere, Michael, like infected cockroaches, spreading their venom and killing anyone that's not in their sphere of beliefs and objectives. If there's collateral damage, so be it. And that's my final word on the matter."

Charles returned to his desk and concluded, "I'll wait until nine o'clock in the morning for you to show up. If you don't appear, we will leave without you, and I with a very disappointed heart. Mister Mateo

Delmundo will travel with me, followed by my two guards, Jack Rymes and Lou Martin. You would follow in the third car, bringing up the rear guard. Don't let me down, Michael Lamont Keller; I'm depending on you and your expertise to be a part of my final solution. Think about it, Michael. Go home now and give my plan your utmost attention and renewed understanding on my behalf. Really think about what I have to do."

Mike got up and tried not to show his shock and bewilderment. *Is this only a bad dream? Did I hear him correctly?* Mike paused at the door, opened it, and turned to look at his CEO, who was stuffing papers into a large attaché case. Little did Mike realize that in the bottom of the case, housed in a special wooden box, lay the Candlelight deadly explosive experiment. It was accompanied by the out-of-band, dual frequency, hand-held transmitter radio. Mike took one last look at his boss and left the office and the building.

Charles Brandson sat down at his desk and stared at the closed door. *Yes, Michael, I know that you are aware of my Candlelight retribution success. Delmundo had his people's eyes and ears on you ever since the detonation in the countryside. But now Jack and Lou will carry the ball from here on out. Either way, Michael, I bid you* adiós *and* buena suerte. *You will need it!*

CHAPTER 30

"I tell you, Beebe, that man has lost all sense of reason and is in need of one highly experienced psychiatrist. His mind is warped, and he's on a destructive path that will kill thousands of innocent men, women, and children. He's a bona fide psycho, evil, and narcissistic through and through."

Beebe rounded the low ornate coffee table and sat down on the sofa next to Mike.

"Let's go to the local police with our story and hopefully get them to put a stop to this whole mess."

"What proof do we have to convince the police that they must arrest Charles? Besides, we don't have time. He and his murderous team will leave and travel north early tomorrow morning."

"So, what's to do?" asked Beebe as she downed the last of her drink.

"Somebody has to stop him, and I've got to try."

"Now hold on there, hunter-man, you only have a shotgun authorized under Spanish law, and you're one man."

"Look, honey, it's personal now. I've been set up, shot at, tied and beaten, and marked for death. And we both were attacked in the city. Remember? Yes, it's damn personal now."

"But, Mike, what about fire power? Charles and his bunch have proven to be a very dangerous crowd."

"I spoke to Ramón before coming home, and he gladly loaned me a couple of his side arms. He has a permit, being an ex-policeman, and wants—no, he insists—to join me to avenge his son's death after I told him of my suspicions about how and why he was killed."

"Okay, I'll handle one of the handguns. I'm comfortable with that because you trained me. Remember, Mike?"

"Wait a minute, sweetheart; this will be no picnic. You will stay here and hold down the fort."

"Mike, if you think I'll be staying home ALONE while you and Ramón go chasing this bad guy nut case, you are truly mistaken and totally out of your mind."

Before Beebe could continue with her argument, Mike raised a hand, let out a huge disconcerted sigh, and confessed, "Okay, okay, Bee, you're right. I can't let you stay here alone for many reasons." He then reached out and gently brushed a strand of her hair from her cheek. "And, who knows how long this chase will play out?"

"I'll be your backup, just like when we were hunting elk and bear in Alaska. Remember?"

"I sure do, Bee. You put the final shots that brought down that big, ugly bear after my rifle misfired. Okay, let's get our gear assembled and ready. Then we'll need a good night's sleep. It's going to be one hell of a day tomorrow."

CHAPTER 31

Ramón parked his sedan at the far end of the company parking lot among other vehicles to hide from the lead car with Mateo Delmundo and Charles Brandson. Jack Rymes and Lou Martin, Brandson's favorite bodyguards, were in the second vehicle waiting for the nine AM departure from the company's main building.

Mike sat in the passenger seat, and Beebe occupied one of the rear seats of Ramón's personal four-door sedan. She was checking all the guns and silently prayed they would not have to use them on this particular hunt. Behind the back seat a large cooler was stashed with *bocadillos* (sandwiches), cans of beer, and some fruit. In a separate box Ramón had stowed in several cans of smoke grenades, several handguns, and plenty of ammunition. He was preparing for a war.

At exactly nine AM, Charles H. Brandson scanned the parking lot one last time, hoping to see Mike drive up. He then looked back at Rymes and Martin, circled his index finger in the air, and got in the lead car. He nodded to Delmundo, who started the engine and slowly drove out of the massive parking lot. Jack Rymes and Lou Martin followed in the second car.

Ramón, seeing them leaving, simply said, "We go now, Mike," and circled the parking lot to be a safe distance from Brandson's and the bodyguards' cars. As they drove through traffic, Ramón gave a quick look to Mike and said, "It appears Señor Brandson turned right onto Calle de Mateo Inurria. He doesn't seem wanting to take the *autopista* toll road to Irun. That is strange."

"Why so?" asked Mike.

"*Quién sabe?*" replied Ramón. "Perhaps the señor feels safer on the secondary roads."

"We'll just keep a safe unseen distance behind his and his bodyguards' car," said Mike.

The journey took its time, passing through small farming villages, on into Guadalajara, and finally on to Jadraque. Beebe, sitting in the back seat, had finally arranged all the food and combat material when she noticed several cans of "smoke grenades."

"Holy smokes, Ramón, are you really expecting a war?"

"One must always prepare for the worst. You may never know what to expect when you are dealing with *un hombre loco*," replied Ramón.

"Good advice," answered Mike.

CHAPTER 32

The roads were now approaching the high country, with Pamplona to the east. Huge cumulus clouds were also forming, with dark grey areas in its base. Mike wondered if they were going to hit some rain later on.

When the two lead cars merged back onto N-21, the old main highway, and leaving Pamplona, they all headed for several known tunnels that thread their way through this mountainous area. With a sudden stomp on the brake pedal, Ramón cursed aloud as his car came to an abrupt stop. There in the narrow road, not fifteen meters ahead, stood the two guards, Jack Rymes and Lou Martin—arms folded and standing ready to challenge the third party. Mike got out of the car, still holding an unopened can of beer. *Damn, this is going to spoil my day.*

"Did you Keystone Cops really think you were not noticed following us, instead of joining our group from the start?"

Ramón also slid out of his car. "Hold on, Ramón," said Mike. He also raised both hands and said, "We don't want any trouble guys, just wondering what's going on."

"And what's that in your right hand, Mike?" asked Jack.

"Hey, it's just beer, and to show our intentions, here, have one," and he lobbed an underhand pitch to Jack. "Hold on I'll get another one for Lou."

Mike reached into the car and quietly said, "Quick, Beebe, hand me one of those smoke grenades." Beebe knocked up the top of the ammo box and handed Mike a can with, "Be careful, Mike, those guys have guns on us." Mike pulled the pin on the grenade, straightened up and pitched it to Lou.

As Lou caught it, it hissed for a microsecond then, with a small BANG, it billowed thick white smoke, engulfing the two guards. Lou dropped the grenade, drew up his gun and, cursing wildly, shot into the direction of Ramón's car. One bullet hit the windshield and another ricocheted off the front fender.

"*Hijo de puta!*" screamed Ramón, who pulled out a six-inch knife and charged into the dense white smoke. He would now avenge the death of Hilario, his only son.

"Ramón, wait!" yelled Mike as he tried to see where the two guards had gone. But Ramón had already run into Jack Rymes, who stumbled back a few steps. Ramón gripped Lou's jacket and drove the knife into the soft belly of the guard. Lou screamed and pulled the trigger of his gun that sent a bullet into Ramón's chest. They both fell onto the hot pavement. Somehow Lou got up and staggered to find his car. Jack was already behind the wheel and gunning the engine for an escape. Lou cried out and tried to hold on to the rear bumper as Jack drove out of the battle scene, squealing tires as he sped up the winding, hilly road.

"Ramón!" Mike called out to his friend. He found him on the road, bleeding and holding a hand to his chest. Mike rolled him onto his back and cradled his head.

"Michael, that . . . *bastardo* . . . has . . . killed me." Ramón tried to raise a hand, but his eyes rolled back into his head and he died in Mike's arms. Mike tried to speak to him, but he knew it was too late. He picked up Ramón and laid him off the road into a small ditch. Beebe ran up, holding her hand to her mouth, trying to squelch a cry.

Meanwhile, Lou could not hold onto the car's bumper any longer and finally let go, and he too rolled off to the side of the road. He was bloody with Ramón's knife still stuck in his side. Lou Martin died where he lay.

"Get in the car, Beebe, I'm going after Jack!" Mike had murder in his eyes.

"Mike, maybe—" Beebe's plea was shut down by Mike's hard voice.

"I'm going to get that sonofabitch, so hang on tight." He floored Ramón's powerful car and sped up the road, leaving the dual murder scene in his rear view mirror. Mike pounded on the steering wheel to urge the big car to go faster, and it responded as if alive. Tires squealed around tight mountain turns, and Mike could see he was gaining on Jack's car. He didn't know how he would stop Jack, but he just kept pushing his vehicle as hard and as fast as possible along that winding, dangerous road.

Mike floored the gas pedal and rammed into Jack's car. Both cars shuddered a bit, as Beebe shot Mike a worried look. Jack sped up a bit, but Mike stayed on his tail. With one more hard collision, he struck his opponent's rear end a definite strong blow that launched Jack's car smashing into and through a low concrete barrier, and it sailed into the wild blue yonder. Mike couldn't hear Jack's scream, but he knew it would be his last. Jack's car went airborne for a second or two, then it hit, tumbled, and smashed its way down the deep gorge as Mike pulled up to hear the faint sounds of metal being punished to the maximum. Then all was quiet.

Mike rested his head on the steering wheel and in a soft voice said, "And that was for Hilario's and Ramón's murders." Beebe was speechless and almost out of breath, but she too breathed a little easier. She didn't say anything as she placed her hand on Mike's shoulder with a comforting little rub.

Mike quickly regained his thoughts and simply said, "Charles is up ahead somewhere." He started the car once more and kept up the high-speed run through the mountain's curves. Luckily, the traffic was light as he weaved around slower moving vehicles. Within a few minutes, Mike saw a restaurant sign and then a small roadside stone building that had a car parked in a front parking space. As he sped by, Mike quickly recognized the size and color of that parked car.

"That's Charles's car!" he almost screamed out, and slammed on his brakes. Making a quick U-turn, he drove up to the small parking place near the big sedan. He and Beebe got out and approached the car. Delmundo was relaxing in the driver's seat with his head back and eyes closed. He was supposedly guarding Charles's attaché case containing the Candlelight and radio transmitter. Mike quickly opened the door and hit Mateo square on the jaw for a first round knockout. Mike pulled him back up and delivered another blow to confirm his opponent's twilight status.

With a small handgun at his left side, Mike and Beebe crept up to the heavy, wooden front door of the restaurant. He pressed down on the handle and swung the door inward at a normal pace. They stood there for a moment and noticed an old man and a middle-aged woman standing behind a rustic bar that faced the opened doorway. Mike and Beebe stepped inside. It was a very bad mistake.

CHAPTER 33

They had no sooner entered when a flash of a strong arm wrapped around Beebe's neck. Then Charles Branson's right hand pressed a gun to her temple. There was no struggle.

"All right, Michael, please do the smart thing and drop your weapon. Do it now!"

"I'll do whatever you say, Charles. Just don't hurt Beebe. As you know, she has nothing to do with all this."

"Kick your weapon down towards the bar," demanded Charles. Mike did so with the terrified looks of the two restaurant owners watching the exchange. What Charles didn't know was that Mike had a 9mm automatic stuffed into the back waistband of his trousers. He had to make sure Charles didn't see the extra weapon.

"Michael, you really disappointed me. I had so much wanted your help. I am not at war with you or your wife. Please understand that. But you keep getting in my way, my way of fulfilling a twenty-year pledge of revenge for my personal pain and suffering. You must not interfere in my journey to destroy the ETA once and for all. I'm so close, and now I have a hostage—or insurance if you wish—to complete my quest. Do not try to follow me, Michael. As you can see, I'll have my gun to Beebe's head. Keep thinking about that."

"Charles, you talk about pain and suffering. Think of the consequences that will result in possibly thousands of people dying by your hand. I saw what your clever super bomb did to just a single truck. Please think about the innocent lives and property lost through your Candlelight bomb."

"Collateral damage, my friend, always occurs in all wars. And it could happen to your wife," said Charles.

Mike could only surrender any hope of retaliation at this time. He looked at Beebe as she tried to exchange doubts of escape with her husband.

"Remember what I said, Michael!" shouted Charles as he pushed Beebe to the open door and, still maintaining his grip around her neck, ran to his car. He pushed Beebe against the car and, while still keeping his gun hand and arm against her, he opened the driver's car door and noticed the comatose body of Delmundo. *Stupid idiot!!* He reached in and violently pulled Delmundo out of the car and threw the unconscious body onto the dirt pavement. He then pushed Beebe past the attaché case and into the passenger side of the front seat.

"Don't try to escape, Beebe. Remember, I'll have a gun on you for the rest of my trip. And I'll use it if I have to." He then started the engine and roared out of the parking lot onto the mountainous road. Charles didn't see Mike charge out of the eatery, get into Ramón's car, and prepare for the chase with a screaming motor and squealing tires.

CHAPTER 34

As Charles Brandson sped up the winding highway, he wascareful to look out at the steep mountainous contours on either side of the road. He also kept his pistol on his lap which caught the eye of Beebe. *If I'm quick enough, I could get that gun and force him to stop.* It didn't take long for her to make the decision. With a fast move, she made the swift attempt for the gun. Unfortunately, her pinky finger got caught up in the handle of the attaché case, causing a foiled attack. Charles immediately swung out a right backhand that almost knocked Beebe out. A small cry escaped her bloody lips as she slumped back in her seat.

"Don't ever try that again, Beebe. Next time it will be worse."

Damn, that's the second time in this country that two different hombres smacked me down. But that will be the last time. I swear.

Mike pushed the big sedan up the highway at a dangerous speed. All he could think of was, *He's got Beebe! He's got Beebe!* That sickening thought drove him on with a flawless determination. He too had his 9mm automatic in his lap, thinking only, *I must stop Charles at all costs. I must succeed.*

Mike could now see Charles up ahead of him as he pressed the accelerator down hard to close the gap. He thought, *I've seen this action in movies many times. I wonder if it really works.* Mike rolled down his window and took the best aim possible, and fired five or six shots at the right rear tire of Charles's car. Within seconds that tire started to shred, leaving smoking chunks of rubber on the road as Charles tried desperately to control his vehicle. It was no use; he had to stop.

He quickly grabbed his attaché case with the enclosed Candlelight bomb and forced Beebe out of the car at gunpoint. He once again wrapped his left arm—holding the case—around Beebe's neck and staggered to a small opening off the road and in between the concrete barriers. He did not point his gun at the approaching Mike, but pressed it hard against Beebe's right temple.

Mike came to an abrupt halt, with his spare weapon tucked in his backside waistband. He raised both his hands high, still holding a gun. With a passionate plea he cried out, "Charles, wait, stop, please don't do anything you will regret. Don't use Beebe as a shield. By God, she's my wife. Let's talk, Charles, and find an adequate solution here."

"I warned you, Michael, for the last time not to interfere in my journey. It's right here, here in this case that I will finally find success in my promise for revenge." He banged the case against Beebe's chest while keeping her under control with his arm around her neck. His gun still pointed at Mike, who was just ten feet away.

"Throw your gun over the edge here, Michael," commanded Charles. Mike did not hesitate, and tossed the weapon over the rocky edge.

"Charles, listen to me, Ramón is dead, killed by one of your bodyguards. He's dead because he too screamed for revenge for the death of his son Hilario. This obsession for revenge is not the answer. I'll help you fight your war in any other way. Let's talk, please." Mike was now getting desperate and noting Beebe's trapped predicament.

"NO, NO, NO more talking, Michael! Take one step closer and I'll put a bullet in Beebe's head and throw her over the cliff here. Then you will know the horror and pain that I've endured all these years with the loss of my family."

"Before you do anything, Charles—" Mike looked directly into Beebe's eyes and continued, "Watch your footing there, Charles, watch - your - foot." Beebe caught Mike's desperate message, and, lifting her hiking boot about six inches, brought it down hard on Charles's shin bone. She continued the stroke downward onto his foot. Charles immediately felt the pain and bent down slightly, loosening his grip on Beebe, who pulled his arm away from her neck and rolled out of his grip.

Charles straightened up and fired a wild shot at Mike. Charles' bullet went high as Mike was down on one knee; at the same time he pulled his spare weapon and shot Charles twice in the chest. The forty-caliber impact sent him falling back onto the edge of the steep, rocky slope. The

Candlelight case went flying a few feet beyond where Charles lay . . . dead.

Mike rushed to embrace Beebe, and they held each other as never before.

"Oh, Mike, thanks for that self-defense tip you gave me years ago."

They then stepped up to where Charles lay. Then Mike saw the attaché case that contained the Candlelight bomb and transmitter. Mike replaced the gun clip with a full load, took aim, and fired the Beretta repeatedly at the case. As the bullets struck, it sent the attaché case cart-wheeling down the rocky mountain slope. It hit an outcropping once, sailed high into the air and finally landed with a splash in the lake below.

"Drown and die, you unholy, unearthly monster. I hope it's never discovered, and would be useless if recovered." Mike didn't know what else to say or how to describe his disgust with this inhuman development. But he did know the Candlelight case would be water-logged, the transmitter useless and at the bottom of this small lake.

He then took one last look at the body of Charles H. Brandson, shook his head, and wondered why this had to happen. It was all over now. Mike held Beebe as they headed back to the car.

The End

M.L. Barbani

EPILOGUE

After the Spanish police ended their investigation, it was concluded that one Charles Brandson had kidnapped Mike's wife at gunpoint—the testimony of the restaurant owners.

That fact cleared Mike of a possible murder charge. The police also picked up Mateo Luis Delmundo for questioning about his association with the entire group. He affirmed that the dead bodies of Ramón Fuentes and Lou Martin were the result of a revengeful gun battle. Neither Jack Rymes' body nor car was ever found, and nobody knew whatever happened to the Candlelight conspiracy. The case was officially closed after Mateo Luis Delmundo died of a heart attack shortly after the police questioned him about his involvement with the group and the death of Madeline Dubois. The Candlelight project died with him after the entire research and development team were ordered disbanded, discharged, and returned to their native countries by the new head of General Products, S.A.

Michael and Beebe Keller eventually returned to America after the funeral and consoling with Ramón's widowed wife. The Kellers began to work on a new family project. They would finally make a baby.

The Beginning.

ABOUT THE AUTHOR

M.L. BARBANI

M.L. (Matt) Barbani has worked and traveled to many parts of the world such as Spain, Nigeria, Mexico, Bosnia, Jordan, and Saudi Arabia. He served in the US Marine Corps Reserve, then in the Air Force, and was stationed in Japan and Korea.

Matt has written three other books *The Way It Was*, an autobiography, *The Transformation Formula*, and the sequel, *The Transformation Formula, PT II, Paradise Lost*; both novels.

He is now happily retired and lives, writes, and paints along the Pamlico/Tar River in Washington, North Carolina. One of Barbani's paintings was selected for the Office of Economic Advisors-The White House, Washington, DC. (1970).

CPSIA information can be obtained at www.ICGtesting.com
Printed in the USA
BVOW071432111211

278049BV00002B/41/P